KING
of the
BENCH
CONTROL FREAK

STEVE MOORE

HARPER
An Imprint of HarperCollins*Publishers*

King of the Bench: Control Freak
 For information address HarperCollins Children's Books, a division of HarperCollins Publishers, 195 Broadway, New York, NY 10007.
www.harpercollinschildrens.com

ISBN 978-0-06-220332-8

Typography by Katie Klimowicz
17 18 19 20 21 CG/LSCH 10 9 8 7 6 5 4 3 2 1

To Debi Larsson

PROLOGUE

My name is Steve, and I am a benchwarmer.

Do you remember in *King of the Bench: No Fear* when I told everyone in the entire universe that I never get in a game unless it's garbage time and the score is a hundred to zip?

I hope so, because it would be really pathetic if you already forgot. And if you haven't even read the book yet, what are you waiting for?!

In *No Fear*, I also spilled my guts about a really humiliating personal problem that almost ruined my very first baseball season at Spiro T. Agnew Middle School, "Home of the Mighty Plumbers."

(No. Not that.)

In this book, I am going to tell you about a mysterious magic device that pretty much controlled the fate of the Mighty Plumbers' football season.

It was a device so powerful that, in the

wrong hands, it could have jinxed anyone it came in contact with in the entire *world.* And I'm not even exaggerating.

Fortunately, the magic device was in my hands. Most of the time.

I won't tell you any more details right now because—big, drooly *duh*—it's a strict rule when writing a book that you build suspense first and don't just spill all the "mysterious-magic-device" stuff right off the bat.

So just "hang on to your jockstraps," as my football coach likes to say. I'll get to the mysterious magic device when the suspense builds to the point where you can't stand it a minute longer.

For now, you need to know that even though I'm a benchwarmer, I do have some excellent skills in football.

For example, I'm really quick on my feet. That's a huge advantage if you are a running back and a linebacker tries to grab your head and shove your face into the grass.

So I'm not a total drooling dweeb, okay? And when it comes to sitting on the bench, I'm probably better at it than anyone else my age in the entire city—maybe the entire world.

End of the pine or middle of the pine, doesn't matter. I pretty much rule the bench.

No brag. It's just a fact.

I'm King of the Bench!

CHAPTER

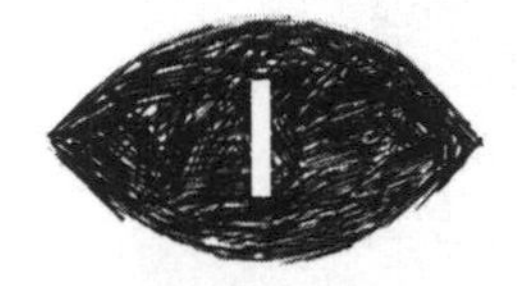

My encounter with the mysterious and powerful magic device happened on the first day of school after summer vacation.

I'd decided to take a detour early in the morning before classes started. Instead of diving straight back into the drudgery, I wanted to ease back into it along with my best friends, Carlos Diaz and Joey Linguini.

Joey is psychic. One time, he predicted a gory incident that became known in Spiro T.

Agnew Middle School folklore as the Valentine's Day Schnoz Massacre.

Joey and Carlos are benchwarmers just like me. Mostly, we sit and watch the hot-shot athletes run around and get all sweaty, which you probably already know is a huge chick magnet.

But we love sports. It's our common bond. And we live in a sports lover's paradise. There's a stadium right smack in the middle of our neighborhood!

When we're not in school or sitting on the bench, we practically live at Goodfellow Stadium. It's got a domed roof that slides open and closed, so it can host pretty much any kind of sport in any kind of weather.

Goodfellow Stadium is really ancient, probably dating back to the early 1980s. My dad calls it a "storied venue," which means it smells like moldy hot dogs and it's practically a rule that you get all teary-eyed and kiss the bleacher seats when you walk through the gates.

On our first-day-of-school detour, my friends and I went to the stadium to visit a friend and to watch the Goodfellow Goons practice for the upcoming NFL season.

The Goons are a "doormat" football team, which means they hardly ever win games. But we don't care. The players are so friendly they often will give you their used mouth guards, smelly socks, and other valuable collector's items.

The Goons are the hometown team, so we support them even when they lose a bunch of games by a hundred to zip.

The morning practice was open to fans who wanted to watch the Goons bumble their way through football drills, but it cost five bucks to get in.

That's kind of a rip-off, although it's better than paying a way higher price to watch an actual game where the Goons get clobbered by a hundred to zip.

Joey, Carlos, and I didn't have to fork over five bucks, though. We entered Goodfellow Stadium in our usual manner: we helped the concession workers unload a truckload of supplies in exchange for free passes and a treat of our choice.

When we were done hauling boxes, Joey selected his treat—a churro, which is a deep-fried pastry smothered in sugar. Carlos went for a family-size bag of salted peanuts. He likes to suck all the salt off and then eat the peanuts, shell and all.

I chose an Eskimo Pie, which is my favorite stadium treat in the entire universe. Vanilla ice cream covered in chocolate. It's nature's near-perfect food.

After getting our snacks, we went to track down our friend.

Billionaire Bill (probably not his real name) is a bleacher bum, and I'm not even exaggerating.

Quick Time-Out about Bill

Billionaire Bill is a gonzo sports fan who actually lives inside Goodfellow Stadium in a tiny "apartment" right under the bleachers. In exchange for free rent, Bill works for the stadium as the official "pigeon-control officer."

He patrols the upper aisles and blasts an air horn to scare pigeons out of the rafters of the stadium. It's a very important job because if it weren't for Bill and his air horn, the spectators would need umbrellas, if you know what I mean.

Bill told us he once was a very wealthy and respected man. I think he was either a brain surgeon or a Hall of Fame NFL quarterback. Maybe a cartoonist. I forget.

Anyway, Bill chucked the good life and now he hangs out in Goodfellow Stadium all the time.

Bill likes to give Joey, Carlos, and me valuable advice about everything, although sometimes his wisdom seems a little backward. Here's one of those nuggets that I wonder about:

"If a girl kicks you in the shin, it means she likes you."

Bill loves being a bleacher bum because he's out of the rat race and in total control of his life.

Next to my mom and dad, Billionaire Bill is pretty much my favorite adult role model in the entire universe.

• • •

When we found Bill that day, he was in his tiny apartment beneath the bleachers. He was rearranging a shelf packed with collectibles and dancing to a song from the ancient 1970s.

One particular item on Bill's collectibles shelf caught my eye.

It was a relic from a forgotten time—the 1990s.

Whoa!

Collectors like me know that an original Nintendo 64 game controller is hard to find. When newer models of the N64 came out, the old controllers usually were tossed in the trash and buried in landfills under tons of dirt, never to be seen again.

Bill's N64 controller was a survivor, although it was sort of beat up, as if someone had been gaming with it day and night for twenty-five years. The buttons were stained a chocolate brown, and the cord looked like it had been gnawed off by a wolverine.

It was awesome!

Good ol' Billionaire Bill could see that I was excited about the N64, so he offered me a trade: his beat-up antique for my delicious Eskimo Pie.

I didn't even hesitate, partly because my concession treat was now a melted glob.

Bill didn't care, though. He slurped up the Eskimo Pie in about two seconds, and I had the granddaddy of all antique video game controllers—the original N64.

Joey, Carlos, and I left Bill's apartment under the bleachers to watch some of the Goons practice before we had to dash off to the first day of school. As we turned to go, Bill said something sort of mysterious.

CHAPTER 2

We climbed up to the highest row of the bleachers and sat down to watch the Goons bumble through their scrimmage.

Joey had a hard time sitting still because the sugar from the churro had seized control of his entire central nervous system. Running is the only way for Joey to calm down.

I told you he was quick.

Carlos scarfed the last of his peanuts, shells and all. Then he ripped an epic burp that echoed across the entire stadium.

Everyone in Goodfellow Stadium, including the bumbling Goons down on the field, turned and stared up at us.

Carlos was very proud of himself. Who *wouldn't* be?

After determining that the stadium was not being attacked by a ginormous bullfrog, the Goons got back to their scrimmage.

But I think they were rattled by Carlos's megaburp because the offense had a tough time moving the ball. The running back tripped and fumbled and lost yardage. It was pathetic.

Out of boredom, I started goofing around with the N64 controller.

I'm actually very skilled at video games, by the way. No brag. It's just a fact.

My favorite game is Bufo Combat, practically the most popular video game in the entire universe, and I'm not even exaggerating. I recently had reached Ultimate-Toad level, which is like getting to the Super Bowl in the world of video games.

Anyway, with the ancient, beat-up controller in my hands, I decided to pretend that the scrimmage was an actual video game and I alone was in control of the running back.

Like I said, I'm skilled at video games, but I had never used a primitive N64. So I sort of winged it.

On the next handoff, I punched the chocolate-stained buttons and worked the joystick with my thumb. The running back dodged and weaved.

I pushed the green button and the red button and waggled the joystick again. The running back—the same one who had fumbled on the previous play—juked and zigzagged.

Whah?

I shoved the joystick forward with my thumb and the running back broke through the line and sprinted ninety yards for a touchdown.

And I'm not even making that up!

I was about to tell Joey and Carlos about the freaky connection between the N64 and the running back, but then I chickened out. They would have thought I was gonzo.

I stashed the controller in my backpack. It was time to go.

Joey, Carlos, and I hustled out of Goodfellow Stadium and sprinted all the way to Spiro T. Agnew Middle School.

Quick Time-Out about the First Day of School

The first day of school after summer vacation is always the same old scene. Everyone greets one another dramatically, as if the break had lasted about a hundred years.

Smiling teachers in every class welcome students to another school year that is guaranteed to be jam-packed with valuable knowledge!

The only other day that you see teachers

so cheerful and enthusiastic is the last day of school.

And in the cafeteria, students slide right back into their assigned positions within the school social structure. Whiz kids. Jocks. Socials. Rebels. Creatives. Germ-O-Phobes. You name it. Every group has its own table.

Joey, Carlos, and I don't fit into any of those groups. We have our own table in the back of the cafeteria right under the "Go You Mighty Plumbers" sign.

It's an excellent location—right next to the emergency exit.

That's a handy location for quick escapes in case a food fight breaks out or a Siberian tiger escapes from a nearby zoo and wanders onto campus and into the cafeteria looking for a quick bite to eat.

We call our table "C Central" because our cumulative GPA is just about a C average. That also happens to match our cumulative APA—Athletic Point Average.

• • •

I had brought the antique N64 controller to lunch. It fit perfectly in my backpack's accessory pocket, completely undetected by any snoopy whiz kids or suspicious math teachers.

I went through the food line and loaded my plate with the "Mighty Plumbers Special," beef Stroganoff, which was just chunks of meat in a milky sauce poured over noodles. It was the only barely gag-able item on the menu.

When I sat down back at C Central, I pulled the controller out of my backpack, but I kept it out of sight under the table.

Then I secretly tested it out.

I wanted to know if the experience at Goodfellow Stadium was a freaky coincidence or if the device really was able to control the movements of live humans.

I picked a random, unsuspecting classmate: Jessica Whitehead, the school genius.

She had just loaded her plate with the Mighty Plumbers Special and was about to head toward her place of honor at the Whiz Kid Table.

Jessica usually has a hard time walking through crowds because she is probably the most polite person you will ever meet in your entire life.

Other people take advantage of her politeness. In the cafeteria, Jessica will be jostled and bumped, and sometimes she will even lose control of her food tray and drop it on the floor.

Jessica left the food line and entered a crazy rush of crisscrossing students with food trays. Before anyone could take advantage of her polite behavior, I engaged the N64 controller.

I pushed the red Start button.

Then I worked the joystick. Left. Right.

Jessica dodged left. Then right. I pushed a C button and she JUMPED over a student who had slipped on spilled Stroganoff and was sliding across the cafeteria floor face-first.

When I shoved the joystick forward with my thumb, Jessica speed-walked—untouched—all the way to the Whiz Kid Table without being jostled or bumped!

But was it Jessica or was it the N64? I wasn't sure.

CHAPTER

I'll give you some valuable words of advice: never let anyone pressure you into doing something you don't want to do.

Here are a few common situations you might encounter:

—You're in Africa and a Maasai warrior wants you to hunt a lion with a spear to prove your bravery, but you're not really in the mood to be eaten by a lion. What do you do? Tell the Maasai warrior, "Thanks, but no thanks." Be firm. Even if he screams at you in the native Maasai tongue.

—An extreme sports thrill seeker invites you to put on a wingsuit and join him on a scenic plunge off a sheer cliff in the Swiss Alps, but jumping off sheer cliffs doesn't exactly fry your burger. What do you do? Lie to him and say, "I'm late for a haircut appointment." Then walk away.

—You're new to a neighborhood, and a group of kids dares you to scarf a huge bowl of raw brussels sprouts, but you'd rather eat live maggots than raw brussels sprouts. What do you do? Simply crumple to the ground and play dead. After a few minutes of awkward silence, the kids will wander away, and you will be off the hook.

Why am I giving you all of this valuable advice?

Because right after my little experiment with Jessica Whitehead, I caved in to peer pressure and agreed to play tackle football for the Spiro T. Agnew team.

It's not that I don't like playing football. I LOVE playing football.

Flag football.

In flag football, players are "tackled" when brightly colored plastic strips are yanked off a Velcro belt. And it is strictly forbidden for a linebacker to grab your head and shove your face into the grass.

But I don't like to play tackle football because I hate tackling and I *really* hate getting tackled. It's just my personal preference to avoid pain.

I played one season of Tiny-Mite tackle football when I was in first grade, but it didn't exactly fry my burger—even with the gigantic helmet and massive pads that cushioned most of the body blows.

Joey and Carlos also dislike the whole tackle football thing for pain reasons. They did not want to play for the Spiro football team.

And we are not namby-pambies, so don't even think that.

My friends and I were just looking forward to sitting comfortably in the bleachers and watching *other* Spiro students play tackle football, while we scarfed all the tasty food they sell at the concession stand—mostly peanuts, churros, and Eskimo Pies.

Quick Time-Out about the Bleachers

The downside to sitting in the bleachers is that you are forced by peer pressure and bubbly cheerleaders into shouting annoying cheers.

My personal most-annoying cheer is this one:

"We've got spirit, yes we do! We've got spirit! How 'bout you!?"

Then the fans point to the other side of the football field and challenge the weak and useless opposing fans to a lame "cheer battle."

In case you didn't already know, that cheer is really old—even older than the internet.

I'm pretty sure it dates back to the Middle Ages when hordes of barbarians roamed the earth picking fights with civilized communities that were just minding their own business.

• • •

But this year, my friends and I would not be sitting in the comfort of the bleachers.

I had just stashed the mysterious N64 controller in my backpack after Jessica's amazing speed walk through cafeteria traffic, when hotshot athlete Jimmy Jimerino and his kiss-up posse stopped at our C Central table on their way to the Jock Table.

Jimmy is Spiro's BJOC—Big Jock On Campus. Pretty much every school has one.

Not all great athletes are BJOCs. Only the ones who use their sports status to manipulate other people for their own gain.

Jimmy, as usual, made wisecracks about Joey's small stature and Carlos's famous ability to burp-speak entire paragraphs.

His kiss-up posse laughed like hyenas to demonstrate their unwavering loyalty.

Jimmy didn't make a wisecrack about me, though.

He used to call me Goose Egg. But Jimmy stopped calling me that after I found out about his secret humiliating phobia that ruined the Mighty Plumbers' baseball season.

Jimmy doesn't want to tease me because he's afraid I might retaliate by spilling the beans about his phobia to the entire universe.

Jimmy asked us if we were going to play for the Mighty Plumbers football team.

Carlos avoided eye contact. Joey squirmed and fidgeted.

I wanted to tell Jimmy I'd rather eat raw brussels sprouts than play tackle football, but I wimped out and mumbled a lame response.

"I dunno."

Jimmy pounced.

That was a stumper. Joey, Carlos, and I looked at one another as if we'd never thought about it before, which was the truth.

Then Jimmy blindsided us with a powerful device that BJOCs all over the world use to gain control over weak and useless people.

He shamed us.

Jimmy raised his arms in the air and shouted:

"QUIET!"

The entire cafeteria turned to look. Everyone was silent—except for a Spiro cheerleader at the Socials Table who hacked up a mouthful of beef Stroganoff because she was startled by Jimmy's raised voice.

Jimmy repeated his question loud enough for the entire cafeteria to hear.

"Well? *Don't you guys care about your school?!*"

With the "Go You Mighty Plumbers" sign directly overhead and the entire Spiro student body watching, we didn't stand a chance.

Carlos spoke for me and Joey when he declared our unwavering loyalty to Spiro T. Agnew Middle School.

Jimmy had peer-pressured us into a public oath of loyalty to our school, but he wanted more. Much more.

Jimmy sprang his trap.

“Great! I’ll see you tomorrow at football practice.”

Derp!

CHAPTER

After school, I went home and checked in with the Power Structure—my dad and mom.

(They sit at the top of the Power Structure chart. My ranking is way down at the bottom, below reptiles, rodents, and amphibians.)

Football is a very physical sport where leg bones can get snapped in two. And whenever I want to do anything where there's risk of leg bones getting snapped in two, I need to clear it first with Mom and Dad.

I knew exactly what my dad would say.

Dad was a hotshot athlete until both his knees got scrambled playing college sports, so I knew he would approve. I think he secretly hoped that his benchwarmer son would someday blossom into a hotshot football star.

Next, I asked Mom.

She was my only hope of undoing a weak and useless decision to cave in to peer pressure.

I was certain she would stomp her foot down and forbid me to play the physical game of tackle football, where leg bones get snapped in two.

Quick Time-Out about My Mom

My mom is an overprotective turbo-hyper worrywart, and I'm not even exaggerating.

I'm an only child. So yeah, that's part of the problem. Some parents of only children hover WAY too much.

Mom isn't quite that bad, but she comes close.

For example, in my first season playing baseball for Spiro, she wanted me to wear a helmet AT ALL TIMES—even when I was sitting on the bench!

Dad talked her out of it.

• • •

I was certain Mom would forbid me to play tackle football.

Wrongity, wrong, wrong.

Derp!

Apparently, football is the only sport where Mom does not worry. Why? Because players wear a helmet AT ALL TIMES—even on the bench.

I was stuck with my poor decision. I was going to play tackle football for the Mighty Plumbers football team.

The next day, at the first football practice, we found out that Jimmy really didn't care about our school spirit.

He just wanted more "bodies" to turn out for the football team.

Coach Earwax didn't have enough players signed up. There was a lack of enthusiasm because the Mighty Plumbers hadn't won even a single football game in the past five seasons.

Jimmy was going to be the quarterback.

He is a really fast and shifty runner and an excellent passer. So Jimmy was the Big Spiro Hope to turn the football program around.

But in order for Jimmy to play, Coach Earwax needed other players to fill out the offense and defense.

Even reluctant players like Joey, Carlos, and me. We were the "bodies."

Jimmy used another term.

Jimmy's shaming crusade had also suckered other reluctant players.

Spiro students of all shapes and sizes turned out for practice. It was almost like youth sports all over again. There was no tryout. Anyone with a pulse was guaranteed a spot on the team.

Even Ricky Schnauzer, who came to practice wearing khakis, a turtleneck sweater, and brand-spanking-new *baseball* cleats.

Coach Earwax sent Ricky back into the locker room to put on actual football gear.

Quick Time-Out about Football Gear

Even though I hate tackling and getting tackled, I love football gear. It is by far the coolest uniform in all of sports.

It requires an entire ritual just to suit up. You practically need a set of instructions.

The gear needs to go on in a strict order—knee-length pants with built-in padding; skintight undershirts made from special material that sucks up all your chick-magnet sweat; shoulder pads with straps; thick socks; mouth guards; gnarly cleats.

And here's the best piece of gear: the

helmet. (Even though you have to wear it AT ALL TIMES, even on the bench.)

Football helmets have cushy padding on the inside that muffles the crowd noise and an unbreakable outer shell. They cushion your brain when linebackers smash your face into the grass. And, apparently, they calm the fears of overprotective turbo-hyper worrywart moms.

Football gear makes you look really tough, like a Roman gladiator with a huge chip on his shoulder.

• • •

Coach Earwax started practice the way football coaches all over the world start practice:

Baseball coaches yell "Listen up!" but they don't blow whistles because baseball is a laid-back sport.

Football is not laid back. It's tough and physical. And the players are wearing padded helmets, so it's hard to hear. So football coaches yell "Listen up!" *and* blow a whistle. Otherwise, there might be rebellion and anarchy.

After we had all gathered around Coach Earwax, he told us the first football practice is known as "Agony Day."

What is Agony Day? It's two hours of running and push-ups and sit-ups, followed by a five-minute water break, then more running and push-ups and sit-ups.

And that's all we did. For two hours. We didn't even touch a football!

But we weren't done. Coach had one more treat in store for us at the end of Agony Day.

At Spiro, there is a steep hill next to the football field that is known as, er, the Hill. After all the running and push-ups and sit-ups, we had to sprint up and down the Hill ten times—or until our lungs exploded, whichever came first.

Jimmy and his posse were the first to complete running the Hill. They slapped hands and bumped chests while the rest of us struggled to finish.

Afterward, everyone collapsed on the field and gasped for air—everyone except Carlos.

Poor big-boned Carlos was still on the Hill. He was on his third trip up, and it wasn't going so well. He wasn't even running.

And then he rolled back down the Hill.

I thought about experimenting with the antique controller and maybe giving Carlos a boost, but I had left it in my locker.

Coach Earwax waited and waited for Carlos to finish, but it was pretty obvious it was going to take a really long time, so he blew his whistle and told Carlos he could stop.

Coach probably cut Carlos some slack and ended the Hill torture early because big-boned players come in handy on a football team—even slow, out-of-shape big-boned players.

Agony Day was over. But before we were allowed to stagger back to the locker room, Coach asked us all to write our names on a list next to the position we wanted to play.

I wanted to find a position that had the least chance of having to tackle or be tackled. I scanned the list.

Defensive tackle? Uh, nope.

Linebacker? Forget that.

Punt returner? No way, José!

And then I spotted it.

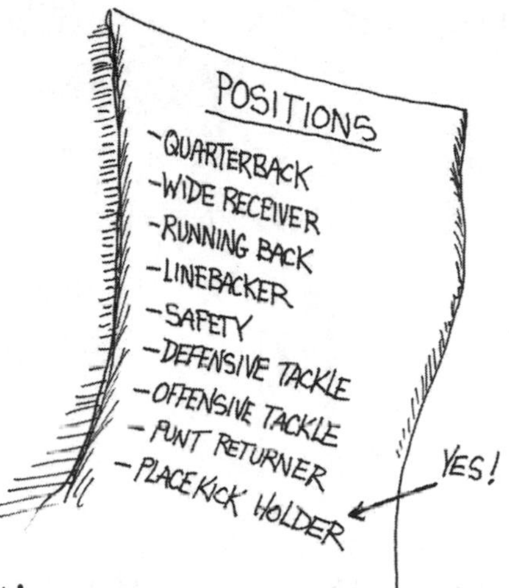

Perfect!

Placekick holders rarely get tackled. And they only have to tackle someone else if a kick is blocked by an opponent who scoops up the ball and runs for the end zone. But if that happened, I could just fake like I tripped on a gopher hole and let him score.

I also noticed that next to the position of “Kicker” was written the name of the most amazing student at Spiro T. Agnew Middle School.

Becky O’Callahan. She has Nature’s Near-Perfect Smile.

She also is the best athlete at Spiro, although Jimmy Jimerino acts like it's him. Jimmy is Becky's boyfriend, by the way, but I don't like to talk about that.

I signed my name next to "Placekick Holder."

CHAPTER

The next day at school, I decided to run another experiment with the controller. I needed to know if it really was magic. Before I told Joey and Carlos about what was going on with the mysterious device, I wanted more evidence that it had the power to control human movement.

My next guinea pig was Carlos.

Between classes, the hallways at Spiro are crammed with bodies. It's like two herds of wildebeest wearing backpacks, migrating in opposite directions through a really narrow gulch.

That causes big problems, especially for Carlos, who struggles with clumsiness.

At Spiro, it is strictly forbidden to raise your voice above a whisper in the hallways, which are carpeted to muffle the sound of migrating students.

Why are we forced to whisper? I don't know. You'd have to ask Mother T.

Her real name is Ms. Theresa, but we all call her Mother T. She is the principal at Spiro T. Agnew Middle School, and she is probably the strictest principal in the entire universe.

Mother T is tiny and frail, but she controls everyone at Spiro with a mysterious mental power that, with just a few choice words, turns innocent students into weak and useless puppets.

After the first-period bell, I hustled out of class and stood on the stairway at the end of the main hallway. I knew Carlos would be heading in my direction, so I waited for him with the antique controller in my hand.

At the far end of the hallway, I saw bodies being bumped and heard voices being raised in violation of strict school rules.

Good ol' Carlos was headed my way.

I pushed the Start button, then pointed

the N64 down the hallway. I worked the joystick. Left. Right. JUMP.

At the other end of the hall, Carlos suddenly lost his clumsiness.

Left. Right. JUMP.

Yes, big-boned Carlos actually got off the ground and jumped over Jessica Whitehead, who was being too polite and had gotten knocked over onto the carpet by one of the migrating wildebeest—er—students.

Right after Carlos's amazing show of leaping ability, a careless student walking up the stairway knocked the controller out of my hands.

By the time I picked it up to resume the human video game, Carlos had relapsed. But the experiment was a success. I was ready to let Joey and Carlos in on the secret.

This wasn't just an ordinary antique video game controller. It was a Magic N64!

CHAPTER

In math class, I told Joey and Carlos about the Magic N64. I was certain they would be amazed.

They thought I was totally gonzo.

I had to prove to them that the controller really was magic.

The bell rang, and Mr. Spleen, our math teacher, started scrawling alien symbols on the whiteboard.

I waited for him to pull his famous "ambush-a-knucklehead" trick where he picks an unsuspecting student to come to the whiteboard and solve an equation that is impossible for anyone but Jessica Whitehead.

Mr. Spleen never ambushes Jimmy Jimerino. Jimmy has hotshot athlete immunity. But I planned to take control of Mr. Spleen's movements with my magic device and lead him directly to Jimmy.

I took the Magic N64 out of my backpack, then I whispered to Joey and Carlos, "Watch this."

I held the controller under my desk as Mr. Spleen strolled around the classroom looking for a knucklehead to ambush. I worked the joystick. Left. Right. Forward.

Mr. Spleen moved left, right, forward until he was standing right in front of Jimmy Jimerino. He raised his long, bony finger to point at his victim.

But instead of jabbing his bony finger at Jimmy, Mr. Spleen whirled around.

Whah?

I stood in front of that whiteboard like a knucklehead for a really long time and faked as if I was working on a solution to the impossible math problem.

Finally, Mr. Spleen told me to sit down. Jessica Whitehead walked up to the whiteboard and solved the equation in about two seconds.

After class, Joey and Carlos marveled at the magic controller. They were believers, even though Carlos misunderstood what I had tried to do.

Derp!

CHAPTER

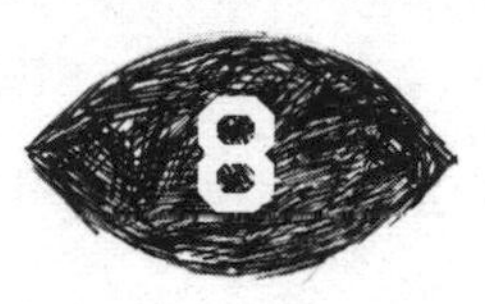

The second football practice was better than the first. Anything would have been better than another Agony Day.

Our bodies had been whipped into fine-tuned physical specimens. Now it was time to get our hands on an actual football and polish our skills.

We all split off into offense and defense. The drills were scripted down to the tiniest detail. Coach Earwax blew his whistle repeatedly so that practice didn't descend into anarchy and rebellion.

Coach had three "assistant coaches" helping him out. They were all employees at Spiro who apparently wanted to show their school spirit while earning some extra money on the side.

Quick Time-Out about the Assistant Coaches

Mr. Mumalo is a stocky biology teacher with legs as thick as telephone poles. We call him "Lead Zeppelin." (His son, Dominic, is the center on our football team and he's also built like a zeppelin, which is the perfect body type for that position.) Mr. Mumalo coaches the defense, and his voice is so raspy and gruff that when he speaks everyone always misunderstands.

Ms. Katinsky coaches the offense. She's a drama teacher who cooked up some very creative plays designed to fool defenders right out of their jockstraps.

The other assistant is Mr. Joseph. He's in charge of kickers and placekick holders—Becky and me. Mr. Joseph is the groundskeeper for Spiro T. Agnew Middle School. He has lousy personal hygiene, but he keeps our playing fields neatly groomed and squeaky-clean. It's weird. He's like a dentist with rotten teeth.

Mr. Joseph also owns a filthy pickup truck that doubles as Spiro's "ambulance" whenever an athlete suffers an injury, such as a nose smashed sideways by a baseball or a leg bone snapped in two by a linebacker.

It would turn out to be a handy vehicle to have around.

• • •

The linemen on both offense and defense took turns running face-first into tackling dummies.

Carlos had signed up to play quarterback, but after his, er, performance on the Hill, Coach Earwax moved him to offensive guard.

That meant Carlos had to use his big-boned body to keep the opposing team from tackling Jimmy Jimerino.

That REALLY rubbed Carlos the wrong way.

Carlos believed that Jimmy should be blocking for *him*.

After practicing what Coach Earwax called the "fundamentals," the offense and defense squared off for a scrimmage.

Jimmy was spectacular at quarterback, of course. Every throw was right into the hands of the receivers. Every time Jimmy ran, he gained at least twenty yards.

Jimmy did everything right. Running, throwing, handoff. He was in total control.

Carlos, meanwhile, had a hard time blocking for Jimmy because he was facing off against Mosi Humuhumunukunukuapua'a, a transfer student from Hawaii.

Quick Time-Out about Mosi

Mosi Humuhumunukunukuapua'a grew up on the island of Maui. He transferred to Spiro when his dad, who once was a hot-shot defensive lineman in the NFL, was hired as an assistant coach by the Goodfellow Goons.

Mosi had the longest and hardest last name to pronounce in the history of Spiro T. Agnew Middle School. (It's also the Hawaiian name for a reef fish.) In case you're wondering, it's pronounced "Hoo-moo-hoo-moo-noo-koo-noo-koo-ah-poo-ah ah."

Once you say it about a billion times, you'll get the hang of it.

Mosi was the biggest student in school. He was six feet tall and weighed three hundred pounds. (He probably weighed more, but the scale in our locker room maxed out and blew up when Mosi stood on it.) And it was all muscle.

When he first arrived at Spiro, we called him "Volcano" because that's how big Mosi seemed to the rest of us runts. But he is nothing like a volcano. Mosi is calm and soft-spoken and probably the nicest, most polite guy in the entire world. And he wasn't a big fan of that nickname.

• • •

At practice, every time the ball was snapped, Mosi would mow down Carlos and chase after Jimmy Jimerino. Then he would walk over and help Carlos to his feet and apologize for mowing him down.

It drove Coach Earwax right out of his skull.

Poor Carlos. He got mowed down over and over again, the entire scrimmage.

Meanwhile, Joey had signed up to play running back. I could tell that Coach Earwax was excited about Joey because he knew from baseball that he was quick as a flea.

Coach was eager to see what would happen when Joey got his hands on a football.

On his very first run, Joey took the handoff from Jimmy and—*ka-zoom*! He was gone.

Joey bolted through the defense before they could even see him, and then he beat cheeks down the sideline. Unfortunately, before Joey reached the end zone, his tiny hands lost control of the football, and he fumbled it out-of-bounds.

Every time Joey would get the ball, he'd fumble it away, which is a common ailment among all tiny-handed running backs.

Coach scribbled a note on his top-secret clipboard.

Becky and I set up in front of a net on the sidelines to practice placekicks. Becky used a kicking tee for kickoffs, but she needed an actual human to hold the ball upright for field goals and extra points. That was my job.

Mr. Joseph had to teach me how to hold the ball. It was really embarrassing because I was a complete rookie and he had to start with the basics.

The very first time I held the ball for a kick, I used the wrong hand to hold the tip of the ball, which is a good way to get your hand kicked.

Then I leaned my head way out over the ball, which is a good way to get your head kicked.

Finally, I knelt with the wrong leg forward, which is a good way to get kicked right in the shin.

Meanwhile, Jimmy Jimerino kept looking over at us between snaps on offense.

I'm pretty sure he wasn't just checking to see if he could rely on Becky and me for accurate field goals and extra points.

I think he was jealous.

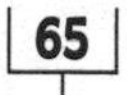

CHAPTER

Our first game of the season was at home against what we thought would be a doormat team.

Nike Preparatory Academy is a private school for students from kindergarten through twelfth grade. The school has excellent academics and one very wealthy donor who pumps a ton of money into the school. The Nike Prep team nickname is the Fighting Platypuses, which sounds goofy but is actually a pretty gnarly team mascot.

In case you don't know, a platypus looks like a cross between a duck and a beaver. It is a semi-aquatic mammal with a duck-like bill, a beaver-like tail, and webbed feet with—here's the best part—venomous spurs!

In the spring, Spiro had clobbered Nike Prep's crummy baseball team and won by about a hundred to zip, so we assumed they would also have a crummy football team.

Wrongity, wrong, wrong.

The Platypuses' team bus pulled into the parking lot next to the Spiro football field. It was not an ordinary yellow school bus.

The Nike Prep bus was one of those cushy celebrity coaches that famous rock bands cruise around in with groupies and all-you-can-eat buffets. It had dark privacy glass and a flashy Fighting Platypuses logo on the side.

The players filed off the bus, led by a Nike Prep official who I remembered from the baseball game. Jimmy Jimerino had given him the nickname "Jeeves" because he looked like a butler.

Jeeves was directing the players to the visitors' locker room and encouraging them with what apparently was their team slogan.

The Platypuses' uniforms were green and yellow with flashy designs on the shoulder pads that looked like venomous spurs. The helmets were shiny silver—so shiny you could see your reflection.

During pregame warm-ups, the Nike Prep players didn't jog or stretch. They marched like robots around the football field chanting, "Platypuses! Platypuses! Platypuses!"

It's a Nike Prep ritual, both strange and awesome at the same time.

Our first hint that this was no doormat team came during the opening kickoff. We won the coin toss, and Coach Earwax chose to receive.

Joey, Carlos, and I were on the bench, as usual. Actually, we weren't "on" the bench.

Football players rarely actually sit on the bench. Football is a gutsy sport, so players are expected to stand on the sideline for the entire game unless they get hurt or come down with a nasty stomach virus.

Except for Carlos. He almost always sits, even though he's not hurt or sick to his stomach.

Behind the bench, the Spiro fans sat comfortably in the bleachers and scarfed delicious concession food. Joey began to fidget because his central nervous system had detected a nearby sugary churro.

Across the field, the visitors' bleachers were packed with the Platypuses fans who were all dressed in yellow and green. Our cheering section tried to engage them in that ancient "we've got spirit" cheer battle, but the Nike Prep fans blew it off.

They had their own cheer.

The Platypuses kicker ran onto the field and set the football on a tee. He wasn't a very big kid, but his legs were really thick.

Jimmy Jimerino and his posse pointed at him and cackled like hyenas because the kicker was barefoot!

I already told you that Joey is psychic, but what I didn't tell you is that he has no control over his predictions. They just sort of pop up out of nowhere. And that's what happened right before the Platypuses kicker booted the football.

The barefoot kicker took three approach steps, and then he smacked the football, soccer-style, so hard the sound echoed in the stadium like one of Carlos's epic burps.

Skinny Dennis was standing at the ten-yard line waiting to return the kickoff, but he never got a chance to catch it and run it back.

The football sailed over Skinny Dennis and the end zone and flew out of the stadium. It landed a block away on the roof of a police cruiser on Seventh Avenue.

It was a monster kick.

Jimmy and his posse stopped laughing. Coach Earwax stopped digging wax out of his ear with his car keys. The Spiro boosters went silent, except for one girl who didn't realize everyone had stopped cheering.

We immediately nicknamed the barefoot kicker "Thunderfoot."

He jogged back to the Nike Prep sideline and sat down, as if it was no big deal that he'd just kicked a football with his bare foot out of the stadium and onto the roof of a police cruiser on Seventh Avenue.

The other Platypuses players were not extraordinary athletes like Thunderfoot, but they made up for it with what Coach Earwax called "smarts."

For example, the Platypuses quarterback didn't have a strong arm like Jimmy Jimerino, but he could "read" the defense and throw short, quick passes to the receivers, who were always in the right spot to catch the ball.

The Platypuses linebackers weren't very big or fast, but they could "read" the offense and figure out ahead of time where the running back was going to go, and then they'd be waiting there to shove his face into the grass.

And Nike Prep players lived up to their motto: "Think positive!" Even the poor Platypuses lineman who had to face off against Mosi Humuhumunukunukuapua'a.

He couldn't.

I AM SORRY.

But at least he was thinking positive!

Jimmy Jimerino played brilliantly in the game against Nike Prep. He was always in control at quarterback and doing the right thing, but his Spiro teammates let him down.

Tommy Hanks is Jimmy's favorite receiver. He is not as fast as Joey, but he's still a speedy guy. And normally he has "good hands," which means the skin on his palms and fingers is like superglue.

But in the game against Nike Prep,

Tommy dropped every pass that Jimmy threw to him.

And Kevin Bruce, our first-string running back, could not get through the Platypuses' defensive line. Off left guard. Off right tackle. Straight up the gut.

Zero yardage. Kevin got slammed every time at the line of scrimmage by the Platypuses defense.

Smarts! Think positive!

At one point, Coach Earwax got so frustrated and desperate, he put Joey in at running back.

Joey took the handoff from Jimmy and shot like a spit wad through the Platypuses defense.

But fumble-itis struck again at the two-yard line and Joey lost control of the football. A Platypuses player scooped up the ball and ran all the way downfield for a touchdown.

After halftime, Becky kicked off from the tee, but otherwise she and I never stepped foot onto the field because there was no opportunity to kick an extra point or a field goal.

Until the final second of the game.

All game long, I'd kept thinking to myself: Should I or shouldn't I?

Should I try to help my team with the Magic N64, or would that be cheating?

With just ten seconds remaining in the game, I decided to pull the controller out of my equipment bag.

We had the ball on our own twenty-yard line. Jimmy took the snap and handed it off to Kevin Bruce.

It was our last chance to score and at least save us from the humiliation of a goose egg on the scoreboard.

I pushed the red Start button on the Magic

N64 and worked the joystick.

Kevin dodged left. He cut right. He broke through the Platypuses' defense and streaked down the field. It looked like he would score a touchdown, but at the last second, a Nike Prep defender dove at Kevin's feet. Kevin tripped and stumbled out of bounds at the five-yard line.

Kevin had to be helped off the field because when he tripped out of bounds he smacked into the Mighty Plumbers mascot. Jessica Whitehead, the school genius, was inside the mascot suit. She wasn't hurt, but it looked like Kevin might have broken his wrist.

Mr. Joseph helped Kevin into his filthy pickup truck and drove him to the emergency room.

There was only one second left on the game clock.

Coach Earwax signaled for a field-goal attempt. I stashed the Magic N64 back in my bag and ran onto the field.

Becky and I set up exactly like Mr. Joseph

had coached us in practice. Becky was focused and confident. I was a little nervous and not so focused.

I glanced up into the bleachers. Because it was such a blowout, there were only a few Spiro fans remaining.

Our guys were set up on the line, and I started the count. It was like being a quarterback who is in total control of ten other players. They wouldn't move until I said they could move.

Hike!

I took the snap and set the football in the proper upright position.

Becky took three approach steps and booted the ball straight through the uprights!

I didn't get my hand kicked. I didn't get my head kicked. And I didn't get kicked in the shinbone. (Maybe that would have been okay, according to Billionaire Bill.)

Becky had scored the only Mighty Plumbers points in the game.

Becky and I bumped fists and slapped high fives. Jimmy Jimerino glared at me.

Spiro had lost to Nike Prep by about a hundred to three, but there was hope for the season thanks to the Magic N64.

CHAPTER

Our next football practice after we got creamed by Nike Prep was like another Agony Day.

Okay, it wasn't *that* bad. But we did get punished for our pathetic performance.

Coach Earwax believed that we'd lost the game because the other team was in "superior physical condition."

So practice was two hours of running and push-ups and sit-ups, a five-minute water break, then more running and push-ups and sit-ups. It was brutal.

Halfway through practice, Ricky Schnauzer got fed up and walked off the field. He changed back into his khakis and turtleneck sweater and told Coach Earwax that he was volunteering to be the team equipment manager.

I actually admired Ricky. It's not easy to say "I'm outta here" right in front of the entire team. But "Agony Day, the Sequel" wasn't exactly frying Ricky's burger, so he took control and did something about it.

We closed out practice with ten trips up and down the Hill.

Carlos showed some improvement from

the first Agony Day. He crawled uphill and then rolled downhill four and a half times before Coach Earwax finally gave up and blew the whistle for the end of practice.

As we staggered off the field toward the locker rooms, Coach Earwax gave Becky the only compliment from the Nike Prep disaster.

It's not very wordy, but "atta babe" is the ultimate compliment from a coach.

CHAPTER

When I got home from practice, I couldn't stop thinking about the Magic N64.

Was it cheating to use magic in a football game?

I didn't want to cheat because the Power Structure had drilled it into my brain, practically from the day I was born, that cheating is wrong.

Mom says people who cheat are just trying to avoid hard work. And Dad would never cheat because he was a hotshot athlete before his knees got scrambled, so he never needed extra help.

I decided I'd ask my ex–hotshot athlete dad if it's against the rules in football to use a magic video game device to control the movements of human players.

But before I could track down Dad, a disturbance erupted between two of my "family members."

I don't have any brothers or sisters, but I do have four pets that can be just as annoying as human siblings.

My favorite pet is Fido, a boa constrictor that will eventually grow to be ten feet long. That's big enough to swallow a poodle. For now, he can only stretch his jaws open wide enough to swallow an average-size rat.

I keep Fido under control with some basic commands: Sit up. Fetch. Roll over. Come. Stay.

He can do pretty much anything that doesn't require arms or legs. Fido is the coolest pet in the entire universe, but he has a bad habit of getting out of his cage and roaming the house.

I've also got a bug-eyed goldfish named Zoner. He has a rare disorder that causes him to fall asleep without warning and go belly-up in his tank.

But the family disturbance involved my other two pets, Cleo and Frenchy.

Cleo is a duck that thinks she's a dog. Why? I don't know. You'd have to ask Cleo. She's smarter than a ninth grader and lives a life of leisure in our backyard pond.

Cleo barks whenever anyone rings our doorbell and howls when she hears sirens. And Cleo is madly in love with Frenchy.

Frenchy is a poodle that's just about the right size for a ten-foot boa constrictor to swallow.

He is the most demented poodle in the universe, and I'm not even exaggerating. Frenchy lives under my bed and growls and barks at any sound or movement. He only comes out from under the bed when it's absolutely necessary to "do his business."

On this particular night, I heard what sounded like a dogfight in the backyard, so I went to check it out.

It looked like Cleo wanted to kiss Frenchy—even though ducks don't have lips—but Frenchy wasn't in the mood.

Cleo can be really controlling. She calls the shots in the relationship with Frenchy, but he doesn't like to be told what to do. And I don't think Frenchy even wants to be in a relationship with a duck.

I stepped in between the bickering couple like a referee and broke up the quarrel. I told Cleo to go into the pond and chill out. Then I told Frenchy to get back under my bed.

Frenchy sprinted full speed into the house.

• • •

When I returned to my bedroom, Frenchy was not under the bed. He was on his hind legs, drooling and sniffing the Magic N64, which I had left on my nightstand.

When he saw me, Frenchy immediately dove under the bed. Poodles are a very sneaky breed of dog that does not like to get caught snooping around.

Just for the heck of it, I pointed the controller at Frenchy and worked the buttons. I wanted to see if I could move him out from under the bed against his will, but it didn't work.

The Magic N64 apparently has no power over demented poodles.

I put the controller on top of my dresser where Frenchy could not drool all over it. Then I went to ask my dad if using magic is against the Rules of Football.

CHAPTER

Dad was in the family room practicing his putts on the carpet by tapping golf balls into a plastic cup. It wasn't going well. He had missed about a dozen putts, and I could tell that he was losing control of his emotions. He cocked his arm and was about to throw his putter out the window, so I did that thing where you clear your throat before speaking up.

Dad regained control of his golf tantrum

and acted as if he was just . . . er . . . stretching.

I didn't want to totally spill the beans about the Magic N64, so I asked Dad in a vague and roundabout way if it was cheating to use magic in the game of football.

Dad couldn't think of a specific rule against using magic in the game of football.

Then he missed another easy putt and I quickly left before a window got shattered.

My dad usually is a reliable source of valuable wisdom, especially when it deals with sports. But this time he seemed a little distracted, so I decided to seek a second opinion from another adult role model.

I went to Goodfellow Stadium where the doormat Goons were getting slaughtered by the Los Angeles Rams by about a hundred to zip.

Billionaire Bill was patrolling the bleachers, blasting his air horn up at the pigeons roosting in the rafters. (The air horn fit right in with the usual noisy racket in the bleachers, so none of the spectators even noticed that they were being saved from a gross fate.)

I spilled the beans to Bill about the magic

controller. He looked at me as if I was gonzo. Crazy. Flip City.

But then Bill repeated the same mysterious words he uttered when I first got the N64:

"Control your own life."

I still wasn't exactly sure what he meant. But I was pretty sure that if I added up both partial answers I now had full approval from two of my favorite adult role models to use the Magic N64 during football games.

That was a huge relief because I wasn't looking forward to suffering guilt pains for my entire life and then confessing at the last second on my deathbed.

CHAPTER

Spiro's next football game was against the defending league champions: Chaney Middle School, "Home of the Werewolves."

It was an away game. On the way there, Joey, Carlos, and I were sitting in the worst seats on the bus—at the very front. As usual, Jimmy Jimerino and his posse hogged all the best seats at the very back of the bus where they could get away with all kinds of fun shenanigans.

I was sitting next to Coach Earwax, who was preoccupied with his usual habit during bus rides to away games.

Yanking hairs out of your nostrils requires total concentration, so I knew Coach wouldn't notice when I decided to practice with the Magic N64.

At one point, we stopped at an intersection where an elderly woman with a walker was trying to cross the street through a crowd of pedestrians holding coffee cups in one hand and cell phones in the other.

She was getting bumped and jostled just

like a running back. Perfect test subject.

I pushed the Start button on the controller and pointed it at the woman. Then I worked the joystick and buttons.

She dodged left. She dodged right. I pushed the joystick forward with my thumb.

Well, the elderly woman didn't sprint like a running back, but she did shuffle a little bit faster and cut through the pedestrians all the way to the safety of the far curb.

She must have gained some confidence because, as our bus pulled away, I looked back and saw her get bumped again on the sidewalk by a man in a suit who was talking on his cell phone. She raised her walker overhead and conked the guy right on top of his noggin.

After my experiment with the pedestrian, I stuffed the Magic N64 back in my bag. Our bus had arrived at Chaney.

The school is built like a medieval fortress. We drove through rusty iron gates that looked like something in an old horror movie.

The gates squeaked loudly when they opened, as if the hinges were all rusty from several centuries of exposure to dark and stormy nights.

As our bus rolled slowly through the parking lot, scattered packs of Chaney students stared at us with menacing scowls on their faces. They looked as if, at any second, they might charge and attack the rear tires of the bus.

And there were crows that looked like vultures perched in gnarly trees with no leaves. And a black cat dashed across in front of our bus—I'm not even making that up!

Coach Earwax wasn't too concerned, though. He had been to Chaney many times before and had never been severely injured. He tried to calm our nerves.

That wasn't helpful.

Chaney Middle School had a reputation as the scariest team in the league. Our game was at night, during a full moon, so it was especially creepy.

The most frightening Chaney player of all was a big, hairy guy nicknamed "Beast."

Beast was standing next to the entrance to the visitors' locker room. Apparently, he was the self-appointed Official Werewolves Greeter.

But he wasn't smiling like a normal greeter. Beast growled and gnashed his teeth like a lunatic. I'm pretty sure he was foaming at the mouth.

It was Beast's way of trying to mess with our minds before the game even started. And it was pretty effective.

We all tiptoed past Beast and into the locker room with our heads lowered to avoid eye contact—even Coach Earwax!

But not Mosi Humuhumunukunukuapua'a. He had no reason to avoid eye contact. Mosi was as big as Beast.

Mosi walked past Beast and looked him right in the eyes. Then he flashed a big, wide grin and greeted Beast, Hawaiian-style.

"Aloha!"

Beast instantly stopped growling and gnashing his teeth. He even stopped foaming at the mouth. He was baffled. Stumped. Flummoxed.

Beast probably had never seen anyone as ginormous as himself. And he'd probably never been greeted by another human being in such a friendly manner.

Once Mosi had passed by, Beast blinked his eyes and shook his big head and snapped right back into monster mode . . .

. . . just as equipment manager Ricky Schnauzer walked past carrying a load of football gear.

Ricky dropped to the ground and played dead.

Everyone on our Spiro football team was expecting that the game with the Chaney Werewolves would be gory and horrifying and grisly. But I had the Magic N64 in my bag.

And I wasn't afraid to use it.

The Chaney boosters were packed in the home bleachers. They were all dressed in black, and instead of cheering, they howled like wolves at the top of their lungs.

The visitors' bleachers were empty because no Spiro boosters wanted to risk venturing onto the Werewolves' turf and getting bitten.

Actually, there was one brave Spiro booster who'd traveled to the game.

She was answered with a bone-chilling chorus of howls.

The Werewolves wasted no time letting the Mighty Plumbers know that we were trespassing on their home turf.

Chaney kicked off to start the game. While the ball was still in the air, Joey made one of his famous psychic predictions.

I turned to Joey and leaned in closer because he is a very soft-spoken guy. I wanted to make sure I'd heard him correctly. Did Joey say "Touchdown"?

Joey nodded his head, but it didn't turn out the way I had expected.

Skinny Dennis was back to return the kickoff. He caught the ball at our ten-yard line and then sprinted straight up the middle of the field. Big mistake.

He ran full speed right smack into Beast's massive chest.

THUNK!

Skinny Dennis looked like one of those big honking bugs that splat onto the windshield of your car in the summertime.

Beast took the football out of Skinny Dennis's hands, and then he walked—*walked*!—into the end zone with Skinny Dennis still stuck to his chest.

Derp! Touchdown, Werewolves.

Skinny Dennis wasn't hurt, but he was grossed out because Beast is a hairy and smelly guy.

I knew right then that I had to grab the

Magic N64 out of my bag and pitch in to help my team against the Werewolves. It was survival of the fittest!

The Werewolves kicked off again. Skinny Dennis was still trying to shake off the collision with Beast, so Tommy Hanks was sent in to return the kickoff.

The kick was a long one. Tommy backed up all the way into the end zone. He caught the ball and took off. But instead of running straight up the middle and right smack into Beast's hairy and smelly chest, Tommy wisely cut toward the sideline.

I pushed Start and aimed the N64 at Tommy. Then I started thumbing the joystick and buttons like a madman.

Tommy juked and zagged and zigged. I maneuvered the joystick in an arc, and Tommy reversed direction, and ran around Beast and the other Werewolves defenders. Then he beat cheeks all the way to the end zone!

The Spiro "crowd" went wild.

She was sort of confused.

Becky and I jogged out for the extra point. We set up, I took the snap, and Becky booted the ball straight through the uprights.

All tied up!

Tommy celebrated on the sideline as if he alone had scored the touchdown. He even gave himself a nickname.

Derp!

I knew the real reason Tommy scored, and I had it stashed in my equipment bag until the next time the Mighty Plumbers had the ball on offense.

Meanwhile, our touchdown celebration didn't last long.

On the first play from scrimmage, the Werewolves quarterback handed off to their running back. His nickname is "Silver Bullet." Not only is that an ironic nickname for someone who plays for a team called the Werewolves, it is also an accurate nickname. He is very, very fast.

Silver Bullet took the handoff, planning to run through a hole that Beast would open up in the Mighty Plumbers' line. But Beast ran into an obstacle. A big obstacle.

Mosi Humuhumunukunukuapua'a.

The two ginormous linemen slammed into each other in a thunderous collision, and then they stood chest to chest, locked in an epic struggle. It was like a physics lesson come to life.

Irresistible Force meets Immovable Object.

Neither one budged an inch. They canceled each other out!

Silver Bullet cut around Irresistible Mosi and Immovable Beast and took off down the sideline all the way into the end zone.

While the Werewolves celebrated, Mosi and Beast were still locked together in the middle of the field. The referees had to blow their whistles until their cheeks practically exploded before the two players finally backed off.

The back-and-forth scoring continued. Every time we scored, the Werewolves would answer with a touchdown. And every time the ball was snapped, Beast and Mosi would collide like two boulders and go nowhere.

At halftime, both teams jogged off the field and into the locker rooms for the traditional pep talks.

Quick Time-Out about Halftime Pep Talks

I'm not 100 percent sure, but I'm at least 61 percent sure that halftime pep talks were invented by a guy who was a coach way back in ancient Rome.

I think his name was Gluteus Maximus. Or Sid Caesar? Maybe Dick Butkus. I forget.

Anyway, he coached a professional team of gladiators, those muscular dudes who wore gnarly-looking metal helmets and battled to the death in the Colosseum in order to entertain Roman citizens, who would otherwise have been bored out of their skulls.

The coach always wore a houndstooth fedora hat, even though that particular style of hat didn't become popular until many, many centuries later. Coach whatever-his-name was wise and very strict. He didn't put up with any shenanigans from his motley crew of professional killers.

And gladiators were really hard to coach. They had anger issues and toe fungus and inflated egos. Oh, and they had a lot of extra spending money.

When they weren't in the Colosseum fighting to the death on a field of blood and gore, gladiators would cruise the glitzy nightlife of Rome with a huge posse of clingy friends. They even had nosy paparazzi capturing images of their night on the town!

Gladiators pretty much paved the way for modern-day sports superstars.

But the wise coach with the houndstooth fedora kept his gladiators under control. He was like a father figure. And if the team was trailing at halftime, his pep talks would always turn the tide.

He'd say stuff like, "Go inside! Go outside! When you get them on the run, keep them on the run! Don't stop! Go, go, GO!!"

Or something like that.

After the halftime pep talk, his gladiators were so pumped up that they'd charge back out onto the Colosseum field and pretty much cream the other weak and useless team.

• • •

Coach Earwax didn't quite measure up to the legendary Roman gladiator coach.

He tried to inspire the Mighty Plumbers at halftime of the Chaney game with some manly phrases like "Fight for every inch!"

But it didn't come across very well because Coach had a bad habit that created an image problem.

It's hard to get inspired by a coach's half-time pep talk when he's been digging wax out of his eardrums with car keys and then he forgets to remove the keys from his ear.

Halftime wasn't a total waste of time, though. We got to eat tasty granola bars and chug a ton of Gatorade. And then every one of us had to use the restroom. Except Joey.

For a tiny guy, Joey has a very big bladder.

After Coach Earwax's halftime pep talk, Jimmy Jimerino complained to Coach about his "role" in the game.

The running game was so effective, Coach Earwax kept calling plays for Tommy Hanks, even though Jimmy was a fast runner and an excellent passer. After all, he was the Great Spiro Hope for the Mighty Plumbers' football season.

In the Chaney game, it was not "The Jimmy Show," so his hotshot-athlete ego was bruised. But Coach didn't budge.

The game plan remained the same in the second half, and the seesaw battle continued. The Werewolves would score, and then the Mighty Plumbers would score.

The Werewolves were determined because never in the history of Chaney had they lost a football game on their home field.

By the end of the fourth quarter, the Werewolves were ahead by one touchdown. The Mighty Plumbers set up for another kickoff return (with the help of my Magic N64).

Tommy Hanks caught the kickoff at the ten-yard line. My thumbs punched the buttons.

Left! Right!

Derp!

My hands were so sweaty from working the buttons all game long that when I tried to shove the joystick forward with my thumb, I lost control of the controller!

Tommy actually had a pretty good run without my help, though. He carried the ball all the way down to Chaney's fifteen-yard line before he was tackled.

We had just enough time left to run one more play.

I grabbed a towel and dried my sweaty hands, then picked up the controller. Jimmy took the snap. Mosi and Beast . . . well, you know what they did.

Tommy took the handoff.

Left. Right.

Tommy lowered his head and charged straight into the Werewolves' defense.

It looked like he was going to get hauled down and mauled, but when I pushed a C button Tommy jumped—and I'm not even making this up—all the way *over* the Werewolves' defensive line and crash-landed in the end zone.

Touchdown!

All we needed was an extra point to tie the score and send the game into overtime. By now, Becky and I had pretty much mastered our kicking routine.

But we did not kick an extra point.

Ms. Katinsky, the assistant coach, spotted a weakness in the Werewolves' defense. It was Beast.

Before Becky and I ran onto the field for the extra point, Ms. Katinsky called us aside—along with Mosi Humuhumunukunukuapua'a.

Ms. Katinsky told me to take the snap, but instead of setting it down in the proper upright position for a kick, I was to flip the football to Becky.

Then Ms. Katinsky told Mosi to "step aside" when the ball was snapped instead of slamming into Beast and getting locked in an irresistible-force-meets-unmovable-object stalemate.

We were not going to kick an extra point to tie the score. The Mighty Plumbers were going for a two-point conversion to win the game!

Hike! I took the snap and flipped the football to Becky.

Mosi stepped aside and waved Beast through the line.

Beast was caught off guard. He charged right past Mosi, and his momentum carried him all the way downfield to the opposite end zone, where he crashed face-first into the goalpost.

Beast was out cold.

Becky tucked the football under her arm and followed Mosi through the hole that Beast had left open—right into our end zone.

Two-point conversion!

The game was over. We had defeated the Chaney Werewolves on their home field for the first time in their school history.

Normally, both teams would meet at mid-field and slap hands or bump fists and say "good game." But the Werewolves weren't in the mood for good sportsmanship.

They stood and scowled at us from their sideline. I swear, their eyes were *glowing red*. At that very moment, the clouds parted and a full moon beamed down on the field.

The Mighty Plumbers beat cheeks for the locker room. We didn't want to be anywhere near the Chaney players when their bodies morphed into hairy creatures.

As our bus exited Chaney Middle School, Beast was standing next to the rusty front gate. He had an ice pack on his head. He growled and gnashed his teeth and foamed at the mouth.

Mosi opened his window and stuck his huge head out. He smiled and made direct eye contact with Beast.

"I'm sorry!"

Beast was so enraged, he chased our bus for at least a mile, biting at the rear tires.

We had defeated the Chaney Werewolves on their home turf, but there was a price to pay.

On the bus ride home, Tommy Hanks gripped his knee and howled in pain. He had been injured when he went airborne and crash-landed in the end zone on the final touchdown of the game. No *way* that had anything to do with the Magic N64, right?

CHAPTER

The next time I saw Tommy was a week after the Chaney game.

He was in the Spiro athletic trainer's room, leaning on crutches. He was wearing one of those hip-to-ankle braces that look like some kind of robotic device. Tony Fitz, the athletic trainer, told us that Tommy had torn the "anterior cruciate ligament" in his knee.

Tommy had surgery to fix his scrambled

joint. The athletic trainer was going to help him with rehabilitation, but he was out for the season. No more Tommy Touchdown.

I had never heard of that knee ligament gizmo, but my dad later told me that anterior cruciate ligaments connect the thigh bone to the shinbone and help keep the knee joint from going all berserk.

But the ligaments are kind of flimsy, so sometimes they snap.

Dad knows all about that stuff because when he was a hotshot athlete in college, he snapped anterior cruciate ligaments in not one, but *both* of his knees.

Tommy looked sad, so everyone visited him in the athletic trainer's room and tried to cheer him up. Coach Earwax even awarded him the game ball from our victory over the Werewolves.

Usually, being awarded a winning game ball is a big deal, but the sports budget at Spiro T. Agnew Middle School is kind of skimpy. They can't afford to just give footballs away for free. Tommy got to take the game ball home, but then he had to give it right back the next day.

One by one, teammates filed past Tommy and gave him the usual season-ending-injury encouraging words:

Jimmy Jimerino and his posse chipped in and bought a cheery book for Tommy, but it was just a cruel prank.

Jimmy's kiss-up posse cackled like hyenas.

And Becky was great, as usual.

She gave Tommy a huge hug (right in front of Jimmy) and told him to work hard and rehabilitate his scrambled knee ligament.

"You'll be back."

Tommy tried hard to hide it, but he sort of got all teary-eyed.

CHAPTER

Before our next game, Coach Earwax needed to find a running back who could take over for Tommy Hanks.

He picked Ronnie Howard. It was Jimmy's suggestion. Ronnie was sort of a drama king who would crumple to the ground in exaggerated pain whenever he got tackled. Jimmy probably figured Ronnie would be worthless at running back and then Coach Earwax would turn the game over to the Great Spiro Hope.

But I decided to mess with Jimmy's scheme.

At practice that day, I made sure that Ronnie got all the help he needed from the Magic N64.

Whenever Ronnie took a handoff, he zigged and zagged and then beat cheeks into the end zone without even getting touched by a defender's pinkie finger.

Coach Earwax was very pleased. He jotted a top-secret note in his clipboard that I'm pretty sure said "Give the ball to Ronnie."

Then I turned the Magic N64 toward Jimmy.

I wanted to sabotage his practice drills and make it look like Jimmy suddenly came down with a severe case of the drooling dweebs.

I admit that it was kind of a shady thing for me to do, and I felt sort of guilty, but my sneaky sabotage didn't even work.

I thumbed the buttons and joystick to disrupt Jimmy's motor skills so he'd slam right into Mosi Humuhumunukunukuapua'a's huge chest. Instead, Jimmy juked and zigged and zagged and sprinted all the way into the end zone!

Maybe the Magic N64 had a mind of its own—and it didn't like my sneaky sabotage.

• • •

The Mighty Plumbers' next game was Homecoming.

Homecoming is a really big deal where students and teachers welcome back to campus everyone who ever attended Spiro T. Agnew Middle School. But only a few really ancient alumni ever actually show up.

On the day of Homecoming, students and teachers wear a piece of clothing in our school color, which is teal. (In case you don't know, teal looks like the color you'd get if you mixed broccoli and milk in a blender.)

Everyone on the football team wore their jerseys, of course, and the cheerleaders were dressed in their perky outfits. Jessica Whitehead was inside the Mighty Plumbers mascot suit the entire day. Even though she was acting as the school's beloved mascot, Jessica still got the same treatment in the hallways between classes.

All through the day, there were special events to get everyone pumped up and filled with Mighty Plumbers school spirit.

We had an "Onward to Victory" lunch on the lawn in front of school. Cafeteria workers were dressed up like plumbers, and they barbecued Spiro Burgers and Agnew Dogs that had been dyed teal with food coloring.

The best part of the school day was that I got to skip last period. That's Mr. Spleen's math class where I go to face my worst nightmares.

In honor of Homecoming, the entire student body got out early to get psyched up for the game.

After all the festivities and the pep rally and the teal-colored hamburgers and hot dogs, the actual Homecoming game was a letdown.

The Mighty Plumbers played A. E. Neuman Middle School, "Home of the Raging Madmen." But their football team didn't stand a chance against the Magic N64, which I used on our new running back, Ronnie Howard.

The Mighty Plumbers were ahead by

about a hundred to zip in the fourth quarter. With five minutes left on the clock, Ronnie got injured, but it was pretty minor—a jammed knuckle that the athletic trainer wrapped in tape.

So I stuffed the Magic N64 back in my equipment bag. I didn't want to waste any of its mojo, and Ronnie's injury made me a little nervous.

After the game, we had a Homecoming dance in the cafeteria. Normally, I'm too chicken to walk up to a girl and ask her to dance because I don't want to risk humiliation if she says no.

But I spotted Becky standing by herself at the back of the cafeteria. Jimmy was hanging out on the other side of the room with his kiss-up posse.

I remembered something my mom once told me: "If you never ask, the answer is always no."

So I asked Becky to dance. And she said yes.

The dance didn't last very long, though, because Jimmy spotted Becky and me out on the dance floor and he hustled over and cut in.

But for about maybe one minute, I danced with the girl at Spiro T. Agnew Middle School with Nature's Near-Perfect Smile.

CHAPTER

I continued to use the Magic N64, and the Mighty Plumbers continued to win. But it seemed like every victory came with a price. I was starting to think the magic really did have a dark side.

With only two league games left in the season, we traveled to play Simplot Middle School, "Home of the Blazing Spuds."

Sports pundits had predicted that Simplot's football team would be one of the best in the league.

In case you don't know, sports pundits are know-it-alls who make predictions about how teams will perform during the season. When their predictions turn out to be totally bogus, the sports pundits disappear from the face of the earth until the next season when they return and make wrong predictions all over again.

Joey would be a lousy sports pundit because all of his predictions are accurate.

Anyway, I kept the controller stashed in my equipment bag for the first half of the Simplot game. I wanted see if the Mighty Plumbers could prove all the sports pundits wrong and beat the Blazing Spuds without any magic.

The game started off with Jimmy Jimerino trying to win the game all by himself. He either passed the ball or took off running. Ronnie Howard's jammed knuckle had totally healed, but all he did for the entire first half was block for Jimmy. He never got a single handoff.

Jimmy was trying to be the Great Spiro Hope. But every time he made an amazing play, something out of his control would happen and the Blazing Spuds defense would get the ball.

The only bright spot was Mosi Humuhumunukunukuapua'a.

He dominated on both sides of the line. Still, it wasn't enough. We were getting creamed.

Carlos tried to inject some game-changing momentum by ripping one of his legendary belches to get us on the scoreboard.

His gigantic gut bomb blasted across the football field and stunned the Spuds players and their fans.

Our players and fans were pumped up, of course, and Coach Earwax even gave Carlos the ultimate coach compliment.

"Atta *babe*, Carlos!"

The Mighty Plumbers' offense broke out of the huddle and practically sprinted to the line of scrimmage because they were so inspired by Carlos's burp. Jimmy took the snap. He dodged a tackler, rolled out, and threw a perfect spiral right into the hands of a wide-open Skinny Dennis.

A Simplot defender grabbed the deflection and ran fifty yards for a touchdown.

At the end of the first half, the Blazing Spuds were leading, twenty-one to zip, and it was looking like the sports pundits were right.

CHAPTER

This time, there was no inspirational talk at halftime. Instead, Coach Earwax had a "heart-to-heart talk" alone with Jimmy Jimerino in the very back corner of the locker room where the rest of the team couldn't listen in.

It was clear that Coach Earwax was not happy with Jimmy, who hung his head and shuffled his feet. And Coach did not have his car keys hanging out of his ear, so Jimmy took it seriously.

Everything changed in the second half, including Jimmy's attitude.

He no longer tried to win the game all by himself. Instead, Jimmy followed Coach's strategy, which he called a "balanced attack."

Basically, it meant that the Mighty Plumbers offense wouldn't rely on Jimmy's talents alone. We would pass the ball and run the ball. Everyone would be involved—including me, since I'd decided it was time to bust out the Magic N64.

On our first offensive play of the second half, Jimmy took the snap and handed it off to Ronnie Howard. Ronnie took the ball, lowered his head, and ran right through a hole that Mosi had blown open on the right side of the line.

I had the Magic N64 in my hands and I thumbed the controller.

Ronnie dodged left and got jostled in a rough manner, but he brushed it off. No drama. Then he juked right and faked out a tackler.

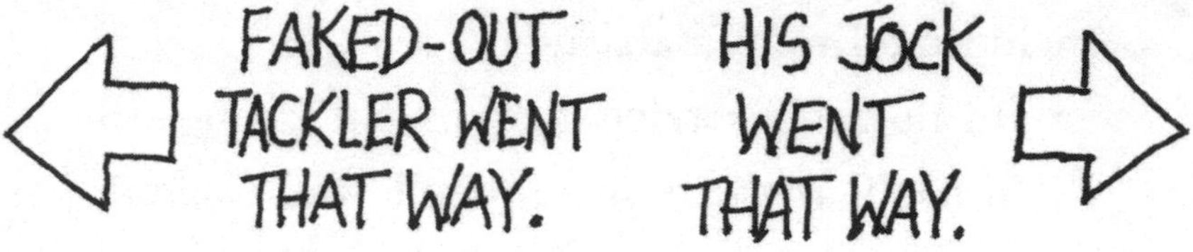

FAKED-OUT TACKLER WENT THAT WAY.

HIS JOCK WENT THAT WAY.

I shoved the joystick forward with my thumb and Ronnie sprinted down the sideline and dove headfirst into the end zone, just beyond the reach of a Blazing Spuds defender!

The game momentum had shifted.

Jimmy Jimerino—the Great Spiro Hope—had made the switch from "winning the game by himself" to winning the game as a team.

The Mighty Plumbers defeated the Blazing Spuds by a field goal in the final seconds. Becky and I celebrated with fist bumps and high fives.

On the bus ride home, I was sitting next to Coach Earwax while he yanked hairs out of his nose. Jimmy stopped at my seat and whispered in my ear.

Even he couldn't get me down, though. The Mighty Plumbers had won the game, and no one on the team, including Ronnie Howard, had been injured.

I was relieved to know the Magic N64 wasn't jinxed after all, but the relief only lasted until football practice the next day.

Ronnie Howard was stretching out on the sidelines when he suddenly collapsed on the ground and curled into a fetal position, even though there was no scary threat anywhere in sight.

Ronnie had been sort of battling a stomachache, but he thought it was from the beef

Stroganoff he'd eaten in the school cafeteria. Now, Ronnie's stomachache had become a stabbing pain in the lower right side of his belly.

Mr. Joseph hauled Ronnie off to the hospital in the back of his filthy pickup truck. Coach Earwax told us later that our running back had been struck with "acute appendicitis."

Poor Ronnie Howard had an emergency appendectomy. The surgeon cut him open and yanked out his inflamed appendix, which is a weak and useless organ that just sort of hangs out in the belly and mooches off of the other hardworking organs.

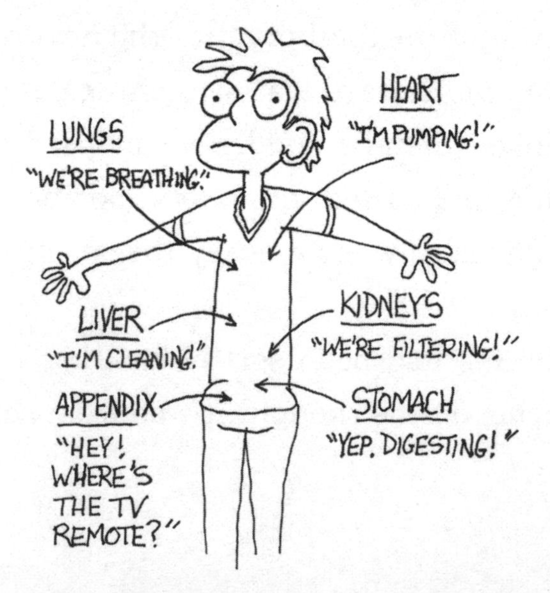

No torn anterior cruciate ligament. No leg bone snapped in two. Not even a dislocated shoulder! Ronnie Howard was lost for the season because a freeloader bodily organ conked out.

And now I was certain the Magic N64 was a jinx.

CHAPTER

The Mighty Plumbers had one more league game, this one against K. L. Enron Middle School, "Home of the Screaming Bulls."

I'd intended to use the Magic N64 to help us win, but I was worried. The controller's mojo won games, but it also was causing painful injuries.

Unfortunately, Enron was a do-or-die game for the Mighty Plumbers' season.

Even though we'd gotten creamed by Nike

Prep, we could still win the League Championship.

Why? Because the Enron Screaming Bulls had creamed the Nike Prep Platypuses by about a hundred to zip.

So if we could beat the Screaming Bulls, we would be tied with the Platypuses in the standings, and a playoff game would determine the League Champion.

Before the kickoff, I told Joey and Carlos about my discovery that the Magic N64 was both a blessing and a curse.

Joey just shrugged his shoulders and squirmed because his central nervous system was low on sugar. Then he made another one of his psychic predictions.

Sin? Win?

Carlos wasn't interested in the blessing-and-curse thing, either. He was standing behind the bench in front of the student cheering section, talking to the Mighty Plumbers mascot—also known as Jessica Whitehead.

Apparently, during the course of the season—and without Joey and I even noticing—the school genius had developed a crush on grumpy Carlos. There was undeniable proof.

With no help from my friends, I decided it was all up to me. This game was too important to lose. I needed to use the Magic N64.

Skinny Dennis took over as our running back. On the very first play, he took the handoff from Jimmy. I engaged the Magic N64. Skinny juked and dodged. I pushed the joystick forward and Skinny scrambled down the sideline and scored.

But he had a hard time putting on the brakes.

Skinny ran through the end zone and plowed into the side of Mr. Joseph's filthy pickup truck. This turned out to be really handy because they didn't have to move Skinny very far. He was lifted into the bed of the pickup truck and rushed to the hospital with a broken clavicle.

Coach Earwax was desperate. He was running out of running backs. With the do-or-die game on the line, Coach put in our punter at the cursed position.

Scotty Anderson's nickname was "Arrow" because he could run very fast, but only in a straight line. Scotty ran in strict geometric angles. No juking. No dodging.

Scotty took his first handoff, and I jammed the joystick forward. He ran at an acute angle from the line of scrimmage all the way into the corner of the end zone!

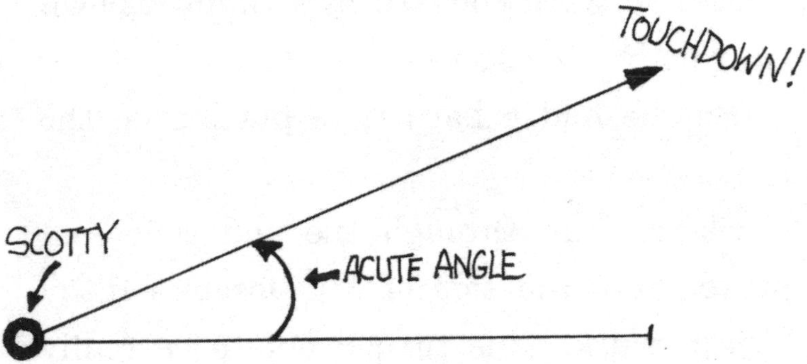

The Mighty Plumbers had won, and we were headed into a playoff game with Nike Prep for the League Championship.

But the curse was about to strike again—in a very unusual way.

Scotty was the hero of the game, and we carried him off the field on our shoulders. He took off his helmet so that the cheering crowd could get a good look at the player who had won the game. But it was like unbuckling a seat belt in a moving vehicle.

As we exited the field through a tunnel into the locker rooms, Scotty smacked his forehead on the overhead archway.

Mr. Joseph hauled Scotty to the hospital in his filthy pickup truck. The team later learned that he had a concussion and, out of "an abundance of caution," he would not be available for the championship game.

CHAPTER

I was done with the cursed Magic N64.

When I got home from the Enron game, I threw it into the back of my closet, which is the only spot in our house that Mom reluctantly allows to be messy.

(She gave up trying to make me clean it because I have a bad habit of wearing the same athletic socks for three days in a row, then tossing them into my closet, where they stink so bad it could blow your nose off.)

If the Mighty Plumbers were going to win a League Championship, we would have to do it on our own, with no help from a supposedly "magic" antique game controller.

I slammed the closet door.

But looking back, I guess I didn't slam it all the way closed.

• • •

Early the next morning, I awoke to what sounded like two vicious dogs fighting over a bone.

When I jumped out of bed, I noticed that my closet door was wide open. I pinched my nostrils shut and rifled through my stanky athletic socks. The Magic N64 was missing.

In the backyard, Frenchy and Cleo were locked in a tug-of-war. Frenchy had his teeth in a death grip on one end of the Magic N64 and Cleo had her lipless beak clamped onto the other end.

They were doing that dog thing where each one yanks their head backward in jerking spasms, trying to rip the controller out of the other one's mouth.

I pulled Cleo off and tried to grab the Magic N64 out of Frenchy's mouth, but he backed away and shook the controller violently, as if he was trying to kill it.

Then he dropped it and ran straight into his "doghouse" underneath my bed. I think he realized that he had lost control of his temper, and poodles hate that.

I picked up the magic controller and tossed it back into the pile of stinky athletic socks in my closet. Then I made sure the door was shut tight this time.

• • •

The week leading up to the League Championship was once again filled with school-spirit events. It was like Homecoming, only it lasted for five days—but it didn't include all the geezer alumni wandering around all teary-eyed because of nostalgia, talking about how they missed the "good ol' days." Whatever that means.

Everyone was in a good mood—even Carlos, who had begun spending a LOT of time with Jessica Whitehead.

There was giddy chatter in the cafeteria and bursts of spontaneous cheers everywhere at school—except in the carpeted hallways.

And nothing got done in class because all the teachers were excited about the Spiro T. Agnew football team, and they weren't in the mood to talk about the French Revolution or Shakespeare or amoebas. Even Mr. Spleen had a hard time blocking out the Big Game and focusing on math.

Poor Ricky Schnauzer got so excited thinking about organizing all the team equipment for the Big Game that he started hyperventilating during lunch.

Fortunately, Jessica Whitehead knew exactly what to do.

At football practice, Coach Earwax made a couple of changes at key positions—running back and punter. Vinny Pascual would be the new running back. And Carlos would replace Scotty Anderson as the punter. Why? I don't know. You'd have to ask Coach Earwax.

Carlos's punts always wobble out of bounds, never more than twenty yards from the line of scrimmage.

The team was so depleted by injuries that Coach Earwax had to pull Joey off the bench and put him on "special teams." Those are the players who run downfield like maniacs on kickoffs or punts and throw their bodies at the opponents without any regard for their own lives.

Joey actually is a pretty fearless guy, but it was clear during practice that he wasn't going to make much of an impact on special teams.

CHAPTER

The Big Game was played at Nike Preparatory Academy's Phil Day Stadium. From a mile away, everyone on the team bus could see the facility. It was that big. It looked just like an NFL stadium.

Quick Time-Out about Phil Day Stadium

It is named after a Nike Prep alum who became a zillionaire when he cashed in on the Beanie Babies craze way back in the ancient 1990s.

Apparently, Phil Day REALLY enjoyed his time as a student at Nike Prep, because he decided to "give back" by shoveling a ton of hard-earned cash into his alma mater.

In Phil Day Stadium, there are luxury skyboxes for the rich Platypuses fans, and the less-expensive sections have padded seats and cup holders—even for the poor slobs in the bleachers.

The stadium concessions are strictly gourmet. No hot dogs, peanuts, nachos, or churros. Instead, they sell fancy stuff like sushi, grilled T-bone steak, lobster tail, and steamed broccoli. BROCCOLI!

The stadium scoreboard is ginormous—bigger than my house. And Nike Prep has its own radio and TV stations with an on-air "Voice of the Platypuses" who comments in a deep, dramatic voice about every little thing that the Nike players do on the field.

• • •

As our bus approached the school, we could see a Goodyear Blimp floating over Phil Day Stadium just like in the NFL, and I'm not even making that up.

Here is actual photographic proof:

Okay, I pretty much just lifted that image from Google and slapped it on this page, but trust me. There was a Goodyear Blimp circling Phil Day Stadium.

Or maybe it just happened to be soaring by on its way to an actual NFL stadium.

Anyway, our bus pulled into the stadium parking lot, and we were greeted by Jeeves, the butler-like dude who traveled with the team when Nike Prep played at our school earlier in the season.

I was going to ask him if I could get a ride in the Goodyear Blimp, but we had to hustle into the locker room and get suited up for the Big Game.

CHAPTER

The Mighty Plumbers ran out onto the field first because it is a strict football tradition that the visiting team always comes out of the locker rooms before the home team.

It's psychological trickery designed to mess with the minds of the visiting team. The home fans boo and jeer and throw churros at the weak and useless opposing players.

But when the beloved home team runs onto the field, the fans go out of their skulls and cheer and clap and jump up and down like maniacs.

Some visiting teams have been known to get so freaked out by the psychological trickery, they run off the field and never return.

Game over. Forfeit.

But the Nike Prep crowd actually was very polite when we ran onto the field. They even had a friendly cheer prepared just for us.

It was one of those sneaky welcoming cheers that are sort of a slam, but at least they didn't boo and jeer and throw broccoli at us.

We got rousing applause from the Spiro fans when we ran onto the field, although the visiting team fans never quite sound as loud as the home fans because they are *way* outnumbered.

But there were two Spiro fans who applauded loudly when we ran onto the field.

My mom and dad.

They were sitting in the best seats in the visitors' bleachers, right behind our bench at the fifty-yard line. Ordinarily, when I see my dad at a game, I immediately get struck with Dad-O-Phobia.

What is Dad-O-Phobia? It's a severe brain wreck that afflicts most people my age. Boys. Girls. It doesn't discriminate.

You can be cruising along in a football game, not making any dumb mistakes, then good ol' Father Figure shows up and *whamo*! Dad-O-Phobia strikes and your mind and body suddenly get hit with a bad case of the drooling dweebs.

But ever since my first season on the Spiro baseball team, it seemed I had conquered not just my Bean-O-Phobia, but also my Dad-O-Phobia.

Mom and Dad waved like maniacs when I spotted them in the bleachers. I gave them one of those low-key responses that say, "Hi. I see you. But I don't want to appear too excited about it."

Low-key head nods drive parents right out of their skulls, which is the main reason kids my age do it all the time.

When the Mighty Plumbers got settled on our side of the field, Becky and I set up the net and started practicing placekicks. Not that we needed to practice. It was more like a warm-up.

By now, Becky and I were like a well-greased machine: I held the football in the proper upright position with the tip of my fingers; Becky took two approach steps and booted the football.

The kicks sailed through the uprights every time. It was automatic.

No brag. It's just a fact.

I hadn't realized just *how* bonded Becky and I had become, but I was about to find out.

While we were practicing kicks on the sideline, the Nike Prep cheerleaders came around to our side of the field. They greeted the Spiro cheerleaders in one of those traditional pregame rituals where everyone smiles and acts all friendly, but underneath the surface there is major rivalry.

I turned around between practice kicks and sort of made eye contact with one of the Nike Prep cheerleaders, who—I have to admit—had a smile just like Becky's that made me feel like I was her best friend in the entire world.

She gave me a sly wave behind her back so the other Nike Prep cheerleaders wouldn't see her traitorous act.

But the wave apparently did not go unseen.

I returned her wave, behind my back, and a few seconds later I got kicked right in my shin—one of the most sensitive bones in the entire human body.

It was Becky.

Okay, maybe. But, secretly, I was hoping that Billionaire Bill's questionable nugget of wisdom was right and Becky had done it on purpose.

CHAPTER

The Big Game started when Becky reared back and kicked the football so hard it sailed over the end zone, out of Phil Day Stadium, and into a parking lot reserved for wealthy Nike Prep donors.

It was epic! The football bounced around and set off at least a dozen luxury-car alarms.

(I think Becky was still a little ticked off at the Nike Prep cheerleader and she took it out on the football.)

It felt weird not having the Magic N64 stashed in my equipment bag in case my team needed a little extra mojo to boost the offense. But I was determined not to use magic if it resulted in a teammate getting hurt.

The Big Game got underway, and our running game actually did pretty well against the Nike Prep defense.

In the first quarter, Jimmy Jimerino stuck to Coach Earwax's balanced attack game plan: run first, then pass. Jimmy handed off to Vinny Pascual on first and second downs, then passed on third downs.

Vinny took the handoffs and ran behind Mosi Humuhumunukunukuapua'a, who blew open gigantic holes in the Nike Prep defensive line.

We had built up a two-touchdown lead by the end of the first half. The Nike Prep crowd even acknowledged our efforts and gave us a friendly cheer as we ran off the field for half-time.

Sort of.

Coach Earwax's halftime talk was all upbeat.

Jimmy Jimerino hadn't tried to win the game all by himself. Vinny Pascual (without help from the Magic N64) gained yardage on every play. And Becky had nailed both extra points (with a little help from my fingertips).

After halftime, the Mighty Plumbers sprinted out of the tunnel and back onto the field with high expectations.

And that's when disaster struck.

The Spiro T. Agnew cheerleaders had set up a "Go You Mighty Plumbers!" banner outside of the tunnel that the players would run through on our way back onto the field.

It was made of paper. It was light and flimsy. The banner appeared to be harmless—like a football player could run through it without fear of getting injured.

Wrongity, wrong, wrong.

The Mighty Plumbers ran out of the tunnel with Vinny Pascual in the lead. When our running back broke through the supposedly harmless paper banner, Vinny tripped over his own two feet and face-planted in the grass.

And then the Spiro players following behind tripped on Vinny and fell into a heap. Even Coach Earwax got sucked into the gigantic dog pile.

Becky and I were the last two players to run out of the tunnel, so we saw the wreck unfolding in front of us and quickly veered off.

The Mighty Plumbers players untangled themselves and escaped the pileup with only a few bruises to their egos.

All except Vinny. He was at the bottom of the pile. And he was hurt.

CHAPTER

Poor Vinny. After doing a great job in the first half, he had to sit on the bench with an ice wrap around his bruised ribcage and watch helplessly as the Mighty Plumbers floundered.

Coach Earwax moved Johnny Hayes from wide receiver to running back. And Becky was given double duty as kicker *and* wide receiver, taking Johnny's place.

Johnny had never played running back in

his entire life, so he didn't know the plays. Jimmy had to explain them to Johnny in the huddle.

Johnny was a slow learner.

The "run straight ahead" thing was especially confusing. On his very first carry as the Mighty Plumbers running back, Johnny took the handoff from Jimmy and ran straight ahead into a solid line of Nike Prep defenders.

Johnny bounced off a tackler and got turned around in the opposite direction. I think he must've gotten his brain rattled in the confusion because he stuck with the literal meaning of "run straight ahead."

And he did. In the wrong direction.

Johnny ran straight toward the Nike Prep end zone. The Platypuses players stood and watched.

The only Spiro player to react was Mosi Humuhumunukunukuapua'a. And boy did he ever react. Mosi took off in a dead sprint downfield and caught up with Johnny at the ten-yard line.

Johnny Hayes was crushed under the weight of his own ginormous Mighty Plumbers teammate.

Mosi had stopped Johnny from scoring a touchdown for the opposing team, but there was a price to pay: Johnny's face was smashed into the grass. His nose was broken. Blood gushed out.

The scene was nearly as shocking as the infamous "Valentine's Day Schnoz Massacre" during the Mighty Plumbers' baseball season when Dewey Taylor was beaned in the face by a baseball.

Up in the bleachers, a Spiro student was so spooked by the bloody scene that he ran out of the stadium screaming at the top of his lungs.

The Mighty Plumbers' morbid, season-long curse of injuries continued—and I had not even used the Magic N64!

Coach Earwax reluctantly put in Joey at running back, even though I think he expected that it would not go well.

And it didn't.

Joey took his first handoff, and he shot through the Platypuses defenders before they even realized he had the ball. Joey ran all the way downfield, almost into the end zone. Then, as usual, Joey's tiny hands lost control of the football.

A Nike Prep player scooped up Joey's fumble and ran it back in the other direction. He would have scored a touchdown, but Jimmy Jimerino caught up to him and with a last-gasp dive at his ankles, he tripped up the Platypus at the ten-yard line.

Jimmy had prevented a touchdown, but he got up holding his wrist.

On his throwing hand.

Derp!

He was another victim in the ugliest string of injuries in the history of Spiro T. Agnew football. But at least Jimmy was not out of the game. He told Tony Fitz, our athletic trainer, that he wanted to stay in, even if it meant playing with pain.

Tony was skeptical, but he wrapped Jimmy's wrist in athletic tape and gave him the green light—on two conditions:

One: Do not throw the football. And two: Do not run with the football.

Jimmy was only allowed to take the snap and then hand off the football to the running back.

Suddenly, our balanced attack had become one-dimensional. The running back would be the only option. Even though Joey was quick as a flea, Coach Earwax could not take another chance on fumble-itis. He needed another running back.

And that running back was me.

CHAPTER

Coach Earwax knew I was a speedy runner. (No brag. It's just a fact.) And my duties as holder for field goals and extra points weren't exactly taking up a lot of my time.

But he was probably worried about my "toughness" because Coach knew since the first day of practice that I was not a big fan of tackling or getting tackled. *Especially* getting tackled.

Coach Earwax's other option was Carlos,

but it was obvious that my buddy's mind was not in the game.

Coach Earwax, in his desperation, briefly considered putting Ricky Schnauzer in at running back. But as soon as Coach glanced his way, Ricky set down a firm boundary.

Once again, I admired Ricky for taking control. He let Coach know that running with a football into a pack of linebackers and getting his face smashed into the grass didn't exactly fry his burger.

Coach Earwax pointed at me, which meant "prepare to go in at running back and get your face smashed into the grass."

At that point, I panicked. I had never played running back. I *hated* getting tackled. And every Mighty Plumbers running back before me had suffered some kind of hideous injury.

Suddenly, my small intestines started doing backflips, and my legs went wobbly. And it had nothing to do with Becky O'Callahan grabbing me in a bear hug.

"You can do this!"

I had lost control. And in my moment of weakness, I abandoned my vow to never again use the Magic N64.

As usual, Joey predicted everything.

I asked Joey if he would do me a huge favor.

I blinked and Joey was gone.

I hoped he would return with the Magic N64 in about five seconds, but even someone as quick as a flea could not run across town to my house and back that quickly.

Unfortunately, there wasn't much time to spare before I would be thrown to the lions—or in this case, the Platypuses.

The Nike Prep offense was on the ten-yard line. It took four attempts, but the Platypuses scored. Nike Prep had erased our two-touchdown halftime lead and was ahead by seven points at the end of the third quarter.

Before I jogged onto the field, Coach pulled me aside and gave me a valuable tip because I did not know any more than Johnny Hayes did about the running back position.

Got it, Coach.

I huddled with Jimmy Jimerino and the rest of the offense, but my eyes kept scanning the sideline. No Joey! And it had been at least five minutes since he ran off to retrieve the Magic N64 from my stanky closet!

I looked around in the huddle. I could tell that Jimmy's wrist was hurting because he sort of cradled it against his chest. He called the play.

"Zero Zero blast!"

My number is 00. It was a handoff. To me.

I looked one more time toward the sideline, just in case Joey had arrived in time to save my life. He was nowhere to be seen.

"Hut! Hut!"

Jimmy Jimerino took the snap and turned toward me. I moved forward and he shoved the football into my belly. I grabbed it and ran straight ahead.

Everything after that was a blank.

I wasn't knocked out or anything. Mostly, I was stunned. I had run straight ahead—as instructed—right into Mosi's *okole*, which is the Hawaiian word for "rear end."

I got stopped at the line of scrimmage by my own teammate!

I was flat on my back looking up at what I thought was a Goodyear Blimp, but it was just a blimp-shaped cloud. I stood up, and my legs were wobbly. Everyone in the stadium had assumed that I had suffered some kind of hideous injury.

Including my overprotective turbo-hyper-worrywart mom.

She hurdled the wall from the bleachers and ran onto the field. I tried to wave Mom off, but I could not stop her from humiliating me.

Then my mom licked her fingers and wiped a smudge of dirt off my cheek with her germy spit right in front of the entire stadium.

Derp!

Mom was escorted off the field by stadium security.

My runs were stopped two more times and then we punted. I staggered to the bench. Joey finally reappeared. He was out of breath from the round-trip, crosstown run. But he was holding the Magic N64.

Or what was left of it.

CHAPTER

Joey told me that he had gotten to my house and found Frenchy and Cleo in another dog tug-of-war with the Magic N64. Somehow, Frenchy had once again broken into my closet and dug it out of my pile of stanky socks. He was obsessed!

The Magic N64 was cracked and gnawed and soaked in dog and duck saliva, although I think it was mostly Frenchy's spit. It needed to be repaired before our offense went back onto the field or I would get my face shoved into the grass—or worse.

Joey snuck over next to Tony Fitz. When the athletic trainer wasn't looking, Joey quick-as-a-flea borrowed a roll of athletic tape.

Athletic tape is sort of like duct tape. It's wrapped on injured feet and ankles and wrists and fingers and other parts of the body as a temporary fix.

Joey and I taped up the mangled controller. But we had no idea if it still had its mojo.

I handed the Magic N64 to Joey and gave him some quick tips on how to use it before I ran onto the field.

My fate was now in the tiny hands of Joey Linguini.

In the huddle, Jimmy looked directly at me. For the first time since I met him in second-grade, when he tripped me as I walked to my desk, Jimmy seemed sincere.

"We're counting on you."

Jimmy had been injured, something that he had never foreseen. But now he was taking control as team leader and guiding us in an awkward, one-dimensional offense.

I actually gained a lot of respect for Jimmy right then, although he sort of spoiled the moment when we broke huddle and lined up for the snap.

Jimmy set up in the "shotgun" formation, which meant he was standing about five yards behind the center.

I lined up next to Jimmy. He shouted out the count: "Blue! Zero Zero!"

Jimmy got the snap and handed me the football. I was counting on Joey and the Magic N64 to guide me through the Nike Prep defense like a character in a video game.

And it worked brilliantly!

It's embarrassing to admit, but when I tucked the football under my arm, I actually closed my eyes. Why? I don't know. You'd have to ask . . . well, me. But I don't even *know* why!

Anyway, I must have just trusted that the mojo of the Magic N64 would steer me left and right and all the way to the end zone.

When I opened my eyes, I had broken through the Nike Prep defensive line and I was running in the clear!

A large and very motivated Platypuses linebacker almost caught up to me, but I think he allowed too much doubt into his mind.

I sprinted faster and scored the first touchdown in the entire history of my life!

The game was tied up with only a few minutes to go in the fourth quarter.

The entire Spiro team—including Jimmy Jimerino and his posse—swarmed around me when I got to the sideline. They slapped my back and gave me high fives and fist bumps.

But there were two important Mighty Plumbers players missing from the celebration:

My best friends, Carlos and Joey.

Carlos was still preoccupied with more important things.

But Joey was waiting until all the hubbub calmed down before approaching me. He held up the Magic N64 between his thumb and forefinger like it was a soiled diaper.

The device looked like it had exploded. Buttons were popped out. The inner guts of the controller were exposed. Worst of all, the crucial thumb joystick had broken off.

Joey explained that he'd worked the Magic N64 just as I'd instructed. But his tiny hands move at the same speed as his feet when he runs, so it was *way* too much for even athletic tape to withstand.

I asked Joey when, exactly, the Magic N64

had exploded—before or after I ran for the touchdown?

"Before."

Derp!

I had scored a touchdown. On my own. With no help from the "magic" video game controller. Apparently, it was all in my imagination, which explained Billionaire Bill's mysterious advice when he gave me the antique device:

"Control your own life."

Nike Prep rallied behind their motto "Think positive!" and drove the ball all the way down to the twenty-yard line.

Three times the Platypuses tried to run the football into the end zone, and three times they were stopped by Mosi Humuhumunukunukuapua'a.

On every play, Mosi flattened the Nike Prep running back at the line of scrimmage.

The Platypuses' only choice was to kick a field goal. The player that we had nicknamed Thunderfoot booted the football, barefoot, out of the stadium.

Nike Prep had a three-point lead with only a minute left in the championship game.

The Mighty Plumbers had sixty seconds to move the football downfield and either score a touchdown to win the game or kick a field goal to tie the score.

The Nike Prep defense had "smarts." They'd figured out that we no longer had an offense with a balanced attack. When Jimmy injured his wrist, our passing game was dead. So the Platypuses focused on our running game.

Not Jimmy. Not Becky.

On first down, I took the handoff from Jimmy and closed my eyes (hey, it worked before). I ran straight ahead, right into a pack of Nike Prep linebackers. No gain. They anticipated the play and were waiting to smash my face into the grass.

I got up and was surprised—no pain! Okay, maybe a little. Like when you accidentally walk headfirst into a tree because you're distracted by texting.

It was second down. Coach Earwax sent in a play called "Student Body Right."

Jimmy took the snap and pitched the football to me. I took off running toward the right sideline as our entire offensive line ran right to block for me.

When a Student Body Right works to perfection, a running back can turn the corner and sprint all the way down the sideline for a touchdown.

But that didn't happen.

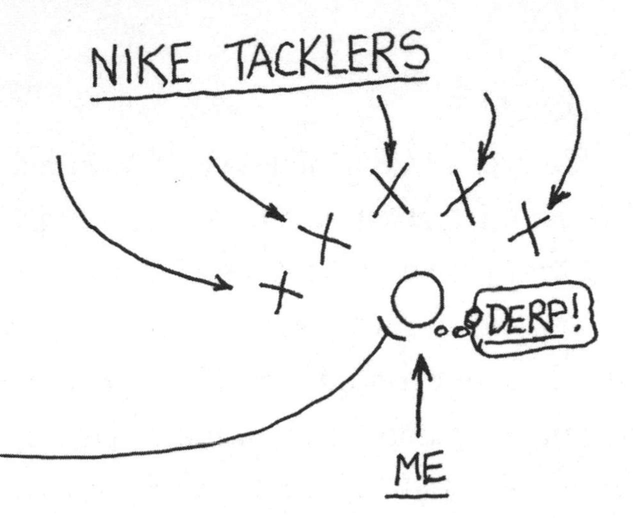

I got smothered. Some more pain, but, once again, no gain.

The next play was "Student Body Left." Same result. Tacklers were waiting. Zero gain. And greater pain.

We were eighty yards away from the end zone. There was no hope for a field goal to tie the game. Maybe Thunderfoot could have made it from that distance, but it was too far for Becky. So on fourth down, with only a few seconds left on the clock, Coach Earwax sent in the final play.

Student Body Right.

Derp!

Everyone in our huddle was disappointed. It was our last chance to win the Big Game and that play was a total dud.

The old Jimmy—the "me-first" Jimmy—would have ignored Coach's play and tried to win the game all by himself. But the new Jimmy wanted to follow Coach's orders. We tried to talk him into changing the play, but Jimmy wouldn't budge.

Jimmy was the one who had peer-group pressured me into joining the football team when all I wanted to do was sit in the bleachers and eat Eskimo Pies. This time, I wasn't going to let him decide my fate.

I had to take control.

CHAPTER

The Mighty Plumbers broke out of the huddle, but before we took our positions, I pulled Becky aside and whispered in her ear. She smiled Nature's Near-Perfect Smile.

I set up next to Jimmy and looked across the line of scrimmage. The Platypuses defenders all had their eyes on me.

Jimmy took the snap. He turned and pitched me the football. Our entire offensive line ran to the right to block for me. I followed the blockers all the way to the right sideline.

Then I slammed on the brakes.

Instead of trying to turn the corner (where the Platypuses defenders would be waiting), I stopped and turned back toward the other side of the field. I spotted Becky.

There were no Platypuses anywhere near Becky because they had all chased me to the right side of the field.

I'm good at throwing a baseball, and I can pass a basketball better than most people my age. But my hand isn't big enough to get a proper grip to throw a football in a spiral.

So when I turned and threw a pass to the opposite side of the field, the football floated in a slow arc and wobbled like one of Carlos's punts.

It didn't matter. The football reached its target.

Becky caught the pass and sprinted eighty yards into the end zone without even being touched by a Nike Prep defender. The game was over.

We had fooled a team with "smarts" on a razzle-dazzle play that I totally made up in the huddle!

Spiro T. Agnew Middle School had won its first football championship since the ancient 1990s during the Beanie Babies craze.

The Platypuses players and fans in Phil Day Stadium were stunned. But they quickly got over the shock of losing the Big Game and regained their upbeat and positive outlook on life.

The Mighty Plumbers fans celebrated the championship.

My mom and dad hugged each other and jumped up and down. I was afraid Mom was going to leap over the wall and run out onto the field again, but I'm pretty sure Dad persuaded her to be cool until we got home.

All the Mighty Plumbers players rushed into the end zone to celebrate. Becky was swarmed and congratulated by every player on the team.

Except one.

Carlos was still standing alone on the sideline. He and Jessica Whitehead—aka the Mighty Plumbers mascot—were apparently no longer "a thing."

Carlos stared forlornly across the field at

the Platypuses' sideline, where the Mighty Plumbers mascot and the Platypuses mascot were sharing a moment.

I worked my way through the crowd of players surrounding Becky. She spotted me and practically mowed down several of our biggest players to reach me.

Jimmy Jimerino was watching, but I didn't care—and I don't think Becky cared, either.

Becky and I slapped hands, bumped fists, and gave each other a huge hug. Then she smacked her palm on top of my helmet and flashed Nature's Near-Perfect Smile.

"That was brilliant!"

• • •

In the locker room, Coach Earwax pulled me aside.

He gave me a stern look. I expected him to chew me out for seizing control of the offense without his permission.

"Don't you *ever* do that again." Then he winked and said, "Atta babe, Steve!"

While our team was getting on the bus for the ride home, Becky apologized for "accidentally" kicking me in the shin when I sort of flirted with the Nike Prep cheerleader.

I told her it was no big deal, and that it didn't really hurt all that much, which was a total lie.

I *wasn't* sorry that she kicked me in the shin, even though it is one of the most sensitive bones in the entire body.

Becky and I sat next to each other in the front of the bus across the aisle from Joey Linguini and Coach Earwax, who yanked hairs out of his nostrils all the way back to Spiro T. Agnew Middle School.

CHAPTER

The mystery of the Magic N64 had been solved.

It was not a device with some kind of powerful mojo that made heroes out of running backs, but with a painful price. That was all either a figment of my imagination or just some crazy coincidence.

There was only one thing left to do—return the antique N64 to its original owner.

So I patched up the controller with athletic tape. Then Joey, Carlos, Becky, and I walked to Goodfellow Stadium and entered in the usual way—by helping the concessions staff unload boxes in exchange for free passes and a snack of our choice.

Joey picked a churro. Carlos chose salted peanuts. And Becky and I both selected our favorite snack in the entire universe: Eskimo Pie!

The Goodfellow Goons were playing the Dallas Cowboys, and they were getting slaughtered, as usual. I was tempted to use the N64 one last time to help out the pathetic Goons, but I knew the antique controller was basically weak and useless.

We found Billionaire Bill patrolling the bleachers with his air horn, blasting away at the pigeons in the rafters.

I showed Bill the mangled N64 that was held together by athletic tape.

"You can have it back."

I also offered him my slightly melted Eskimo Pie, because I felt bad about ruining his antique video game controller.

Billionaire Bill is no dummy. He knows a good deal when he sees it. He took back the N64 and accepted my delicious Eskimo Pie without hesitation.

Joey, Carlos, Becky, and I left him to his pigeon duties. As we walked away, I turned and looked back.

Bill was fiddling with the N64's buttons and joystick.

At that very moment, down on the football field, the Goodfellow Goons running back took a handoff from the quarterback. He juked left. He dodged right. Then the running back sprinted ninety yards for a touchdown.

And I'm not even making that up!

Billionaire Bill turned toward me. He had a smudge of Eskimo Pie on his cheek that my mom would have wiped off with her germy spit.

Bill gave me a wink and a sly smile. Then he broke into a wild and crazy touchdown dance.

EPILOGUE

So I wasn't exactly the hotshot athlete hero of the Big Game, but I did take control of my life and make the most of an opportunity—and without the help of the mysterious N64.

Anyway, I don't even want to be a hotshot athlete hero. I'm okay with sitting on the pine.

I'm probably better at it than anyone else my age in the entire universe. End of the bench. Middle of the bench. Doesn't matter.

I'm King of the Bench!

No brag. It's just a fact.